Broken Sky

#2

Broken Sky

#2

Chris Wooding

Cover and illustrations by Steve Kyte

AN
APPLE
PAPERBACK

SCHOLASTIC INC.
New York Toronto London Auckland Sydney
Mexico City New Delhi Hong Kong

ISBN 0-439-12864-1

All rights reserved. Published by Scholastic Inc., 555 Broadway, New York, NY 10012, by arrangement with Scholastic Ltd.

12 11 10 9 8 7 6 5 4 3   0 1 2 3 4 5/0

Printed in the U.S.A.   40
First Scholastic printing, July 2000

Broken Sky

Act One
Part Four

Broken Sky

KING
MACAAN

MORACQ

TOCHAA

PRINCESS
AURIN

1

Weights and Counterweights

"*You*," said Kia, pointing an accusing finger at Elani, then moving it towards Hochi and Gerdi. "Or you, or you." Her voice was icy calm, but tinted with a quiet menace. "One of you is going to tell us everything, and tell us *now*."

Ryushi looked in amazement at his sister. The others were no less taken aback. He still couldn't get used to the radical change in Kia's personality since the destruction of Osaka Stud. But that aside, he agreed with her sentiments. He was confused, and afraid, and didn't know who to trust; and he couldn't begin to get his feet back under him until he had solid ground to stand on. Before they could even start to get over the tragedies they had witnessed, they needed stability. And they needed answers.

Kia leaned towards Elani, her face a mask of shifting shadows in the light of the firepit that blazed between them. "How about *you*?" she asked. Elani looked like she was on the verge of tears.

"Kia, you're scaring her," Ryushi said.

His sister ignored him. Elani trembled. Everyone else stayed silent.

"Now, Elani, I want you to answer me straight," Kia said slowly. "I want to know where this place is that you've brought us. Let's start with that."

Elani swallowed, and looked to Hochi.

"Don't look at him," Kia snapped. "Tell *me*."

"Kia —" Ryushi began, but she held out a hand to shut him up, without taking her gaze from Elani.

"Tweentime," she said in a small voice.

"What?" Kia prompted.

"*Tweentime*," Elani said louder, her face becoming childishly defiant. "The people who live here are Kirins, and they call it *Kirin Taq*, but *I* call it Tweentime. O*kay*?"

Kia sat back. "Okay," she said more gently. "Now we're getting somewhere."

*   *   *

Ryushi had not known where he was immediately following the moment that the sky suddenly went dark. One second, they had been on the hot, sweaty streets of Tusami City, where the walls were of grey rock and iron; the next they were standing in the midst of a city of sleek black stone, and the sky overhead was not the azure blue of a hot Dominions summer day, but a velvety purple. The sun was no longer bright, but rather it was in a state of eclipse, with only a blazing corona surrounding the dark disc of its center. It was cool, the temperature of a summer's night, and torches burned in their brackets along the alley, the kind that used to be used in the Dominions before glowstones were discovered.

Kia and Ryushi were struck dumb by what they had just experienced. Was this what the world outside Osaka Stud was like, the one their father had warned them about? A catalog of impossible and confusing incidents that made a mockery of everything they had learned during their sheltered upbringing?

The bustling world of Tusami City had disappeared. No longer were the streets crowded with a constant flow of traffic, with people from all corners of the Dominions jockeying for space. Here, the streets were quieter, even peaceful. At each end of the alley, they saw passersby, strange folk with skin that was a dark grey, like ash, and disconcerting eyes with cream-colored irises swimming in a sea of white. Their hair, Ryushi observed numbly, tended to be shades of red or blue or silver; but the color was natural, not dyed as was the fashion in the Dominions. He briefly saw one of them riding on the back of an odd, leathery-skinned, two-legged beast that stood semi-upright, with small, vestigial front limbs held across its chest. He stood there, gawking, unnoticed in the alleyway, until he felt a rough hand on his arm and was tugged back to where the others were pressed into the shadows.

"Don't let them see you!" Hochi hissed in his ear.

"But —"

"*Sssh!*"

Hochi indicated for the rest of them to be quiet, too, and then led them onward, keeping out of sight. He didn't seem quite sure of his route anymore; and eventually Elani gave an impatient tut and, pouting, took the lead. She appeared to know the city far better than Hochi, and headed through the alleys and streets as if she'd walked them all her life. Under her guidance, they had no trouble avoiding the grey-skinned people of the city, especially as the streets were so sparsely travelled.

As they moved through this new and unfamiliar place, Ryushi noted that the architecture was completely different from anything he had ever seen before. Rather than the towering, ugly metal constructions that he was familiar with, he saw curves and arches, smooth lines, all made of a strange black stone that threw back the flickering light of the torches in a shiver of tiny flames. There were no hard edges to the architecture; everything was rounded.

What is *this place?* he thought.

Eventually, Elani paused at what looked like a wine cellar, a pair of storm doors nestling around the side of a tall, elegant building from which came the sounds of merriment. After first checking that there was nobody around, she knocked on the cellar door.

It was opened a moment later by a small, shrunken old man wearing a purple silk robe. He was a native of this place; his cream-on-white eyes squinted at them curiously, then widened slightly as he saw the little girl.

"Is Tochaa here?" she asked innocently.

"Elani?" the old man exclaimed, then looked sharply at the others. "Come in off the streets, you fools," he said, ushering them past him. They hurried down the short set of stairs into the cellar. When they were all through, the old man stepped outside and closed the doors behind him. They heard the click of a padlock and the rattle of a key.

"It's alright," Elani said in response to Kia's alarmed stare. "We can trust him. His name's Moracq. He's my friend."

The "cellar" was in fact a large and fully furnished living quarters. In one corner, a desk sat by a bookshelf brimming with leather-bound volumes. In another, a paper screen cordoned off the bathroom area. But the bulk of the room was taken up by a series of wicker mats, arranged around a pit of glowing coals in the center of the room. Torches burned all around, but they gave off no smoke. Vents circulated air from outside.

They sat down on the mats, and that was when Kia had decided enough was enough. She had had it with confusion. She wanted answers.

Now Elani glared at Kia, her face a mixture of anger, childish defiance, and fear. But Kia sat back, letting off the pressure a little.

"Tweentime," she said. "That's a start. Now I want somebody to explain the rest."

"Look, girl, Elani's a *Resonant*, okay?" Gerdi said, springing belligerently to her defense. "Isn't it obvious?"

Hochi held out a hand to restrain him. "They don't know about Resonants, Gerdi. They've had a very sheltered upbringing." He turned back to them. "I imagine Banto would have educated you in all these matters before you came of age, if he . . . if it hadn't been this way."

The mention of their father passed them by. Kia and Ryushi both seemed to have developed a temporary mental blind spot where he was concerned, a defense against the grief that threatened to break them down.

"So what's a Resonant?" Kia asked.

"I suppose you were taught about your spirit-stones at some point?" Hochi said, answering her question with another question. "That the stones form a bridge between the power of the earth and where you're sending it?"

Kia nodded assent. "Everyone's taught that."

"Well, a Resonant is a bridge between worlds. Specifically, our world of the Dominions and this place, which Elani calls Tweentime."

"No, that's not *right*," Elani said petulantly. "Hochi, you never explain things right." She turned to the others, pausing to shoot an acid glance at Kia. "This world is still *our* world. It's just . . . in between. We haven't *gone* anywhere. This is the same location as Tusami City. We're still in the same place. It's just a flipside. Like a coin. Or a *mirror*."

Ryushi shook his head. "You're not making sense, El."

"Okay," she said, her hands becoming animated as she tried to explain herself. "Imagine a clock. Tick-tock, tick-tock. Get it?"

"Uuuh . . . yeah," Ryushi said uncertainly.

"Now imagine that our world, the Dominions, imagine that they're the first beat. *Tick.* All the stuff that we see and do, everything. It's all in that first beat. But the thing is, everything needs to be *balanced.* Good and bad, light and dark . . . it's the way of the universe. Weights and counterweights. You see?"

Ryushi looked puzzled, but Kia said: "I remember Ty telling me about that. Something the great philosopher Muachi once said. He always used to quote him." The remembrance of her friend brought a pain that she quickly shovelled aside.

"So anyway," Elani continued. "This place is the flip-side of ours. A mirror-world. The balance. The *tock* in our *tick.* This place exists *between* the seconds of our lives, just like the Dominions exists between the seconds of *these* people's lives. Tweentime."

"And Resonants can flip between them," added Gerdi. "Like skipping half a beat. Jump from the *tick* to the *tock.* They call it *shifting.* And they can bring others with 'em, like Elani did."

Ryushi was struggling to grasp it all. "So, you're saying this place is the *opposite* of our own world?"

"No," Elani said, waving her hands. "No, it's just like . . . the person on the other end of a seesaw. To provide the balance. But they're *connected*. Everything's connected. A lot of things are the same here, and a lot of things are different."

There was a pregnant silence for a moment. The glow of the coals threw menacing underlights on their faces. Ryushi looked at Elani, and thought for a moment that she looked much older than her eight winters.

"Are we safe here?" he asked. "In Tweentime, or Kirin Taq, or whatever you call it?"

"No," Elani said. "It's worse here."

"Oh, good," Kia muttered sarcastically.

Elani shot her a look. "The Princess Aurin rules here," she said. "That's Macaan's daughter. If they catch outlanders like us, people from the Dominions, they'll turn us in."

"Or lynch us," Hochi said sourly.

"His daughter?" Ryushi exclaimed. "King Macaan doesn't have a daughter! And besides, he's of the Dominion-folk. Why would his daughter be ruling this place?"

"Nobody knows *what* he is," Hochi said. "The few

people who have seen him couldn't tell whether he was from here or from the Dominions. Maybe he's a half-breed. We don't know." He looked around them. "What we do know is that he is either a Resonant himself or that he has Resonants at his command."

"He can come after us?" Kia asked, without the least fear in her voice.

"It's unlikely he'll bother," Hochi said. "Once he's worked out we've escaped, he'll send word to Aurin. She'll shut this city down until we're found. We have to be out of here by then."

There was a dark silence as the gravity of his words settled on them like a heavy shroud. Then Kia ran her hand through her red hair and sighed. "Okay, Hochi. Tell us what Parakka know, and what it's got to do with us."

Hochi glanced at her, then looked deep into the coals. For a moment, she thought he wasn't going to answer her; he'd been acting strangely towards her ever since the incident with the golem at the mountain market. She remembered the anger in his voice as he shouted at her that there were innocent people about. Ryushi had thought that she couldn't hear, but she could. And it still hadn't stopped her. When she looked at Hochi, she had a funny feeling that he *knew* that.

But then he did speak, his voice coming suddenly,

low and sorrowful. "Elani came to me a season ago. She was picked up by one of our recruiting scouts, wandering, and brought to me. She asked if I could hide her."

"Why?" Ryushi asked.

"Because —" Hochi and Elani both started at the same time; but it was Hochi who carried on. "Because King Macaan has been quietly 'disappearing' Resonants for the last two years now. And Elani is one of the few who are still free."

"Disappearing?" Kia said. "You mean kidnapping."

Hochi nodded. "Exactly. We estimate that it must have taken an enormous amount of money and effort for him to round up all the Resonants in the Dominions. What we don't understand is *why*. We've been trying to find out."

"Wait," said Kia. "I'm getting this now. So you figured that Tusami City was too dangerous to hide Elani, so you sent her to Osaka Stud because it was isolated and safe?"

"We held on to her at Tusami City for a while, but then Macaan started getting too close. Your father volunteered to take her," Hochi said. "Your home has been a safehouse for Parakka equipment and people for many years, since before you were even born."

Kia didn't even blink at this. It seemed that nothing could shock her anymore. Instead, she looked levelly at

Elani. "And that's why they destroyed our home. To get her."

"No!" Hochi said firmly. "There was no way they could have known on their own; we were too careful. No, we were betrayed. And whoever told them about Elani would also have told them about your father's involvement in Parakka, and mine, and who knows what else! From the moment the King found out, we were all traitors. They would have destroyed your home even if Elani *hadn't* been there."

There was silence again. But in the midst of the silence came a sniffing, and then a sobbing. Elani was crying. "I'm sorry," she said tearfully. "I didn't know what would happen. I was just *scared*."

Gerdi put a companionly arm around her. "It's alright, it's okay, it wasn't your fault. *Was* it?" He addressed this last to Kia and Ryushi. Ryushi murmured agreement, too shocked to think. Kia didn't answer at all, just kept gazing at Elani with iron eyes.

After a time, Ryushi said: "Elani, remember yesterday? When I found you in Mother's room with that . . . thing? The thing with the rags and the claws? What was it?"

Gerdi fielded that one for her. "Sounds like *Jachyra*."

Elani nodded, sniffing wetly.

"The Jachyra. King Macaan's secret police," Hochi

said. "We don't know much about them; only that he's been using them to track down the Resonants. They can travel through —"

"Mirrors," Kia finished suddenly. "They travel through mirrors. That's why Elani wouldn't have any in her room."

"Mirrors?" Ryushi said. "Nobody believes *that* old wives' tale. And that wasn't a Jachyra! The Jachyra are invisible. They walk among us, listening to what we —"

"Stop that!" Hochi snapped. "It's just those kind of rumors that keeps the people afraid and the King in power. They see through *mirrors*. Or any decently reflective surface, come to that. If everybody knew that, instead of believing the wild tales that get spread, anyone could plot treason in secret and the King would be none the wiser. All they'd have to do is make sure they couldn't be seen by the Jachyra. But they *don't* know that, and we don't have the manpower to educate them."

"That's how they find you," Elani whispered, brushing her smooth black hair back from her face. "They can *see* you, if they're looking in the right place. Through the mirrors."

Ryushi supported his forehead with his hand despairingly. "This is too much to take right now . . ." he said.

"I know," Hochi replied. "You need rest, you need time to grieve. You've done your father proud, both of you. Many others would have crumbled before now. But you need to hold on just a little longer, until we can get to Gar Jenna."

"What's that?" Kia asked.

"The headquarters of Parakka. You can decide there what you want to do next. We'll have to get Elani to take us back into the Dominions, once we've got away from this place."

"Why?" Ryushi asked, realizing the answer to his own question as he voiced it.

"'Cause Gar Jenna doesn't *exist* over here," provided Elani condescendingly.

"But what if it's been —" Gerdi began, but Hochi cut him off.

"Whether it's been found or not, we have to regroup with the others, and that'll be where they head for. We don't have a choice."

There was the rattling of a padlock, the sound of a key scratching, and the storm doors opened. Moracq reappeared, with a surprisingly lithe step for one so old; and with him came a tall, lean, youthful-looking man, who Kia and Ryushi presumed to be Tochaa. He had the same ash-grey skin and light eyes of his race, with a long scalp-lock of dark blue hair, and was wearing loose garments of black silk trimmed with gold. A small silver pendant dangled at his throat. Shutting the storm doors behind him and locking them, he came over and sat down on one of the wicker mats with them. Moracq retreated to the desk and began to scribble with a quill on some parchment.

"Elani," Tochaa said, bowing his head towards the girl. "I didn't expect to see you back so soon."

She shrugged, smiling winningly, her tears already forgotten.

"And greetings to you, Hochi. When I told you to call on me whenever you needed my help, I admit I did not think the offer would be taken up so swiftly."

Hochi grunted neutrally, uncommunicative. Elani gave him an odd glance and then turned back to the newcomer. "Things have gone bad for Parakka, Uncle Tochaa." Ryushi looked up in brief surprise; *another* uncle? But Elani continued: "We got trapped in Tusami City, so I brought us over to Tweentime. We thought we'd have a better chance getting out on this side."

"Since Elani's been around to bring us over, we've been trying to start up a branch of Parakka over here," Gerdi muttered aside to Ryushi and Kia. "Elani put us on to Tochaa, but at the moment he's pretty much our only contact in Kirin Taq."

The grey-skinned man overheard him, and smiled

faintly. "Sadly, my friends," he said, addressing Kia and Ryushi, "the King's daughter, Princess Aurin, has this place firmly under her control. There is not the potential for revolution that you seem to have. But we are working to change that." He shifted his position on the wicker mat, getting himself comfortable. "After all," he added, "we like her just as little as you like your King."

"The King doesn't have a *daughter*!" Ryushi protested again. "Everyone would've known about it!"

"How many people in the Dominions know about Kirin Taq?" Tochaa replied. "Very few, I imagine. From what Elani has told me, the Resonants have always been closemouthed about their abilities — and Kirin Taq — for their own protection, even before Macaan started rounding them up."

"I guess Macaan would execute anyone who even mentioned Kirin Taq," Gerdi ventured. "And with everyone afraid of the Jachyra and what they might overhear . . . nobody would talk about it even if they knew."

He looked at Ryushi. "Besides, it's not as if you *would* know anything about it, with living in the mountains and all."

"They say that Kirins are people from across the sea,"

Elani added, with a touch of amusement. "That they're pirates, who have ships and maps that can negotiate Deepwater and outrun the creatures there."

"Macaan plays on the fears of the people," Tochaa agreed. "We don't know what's out beyond the great oceans, so superstition is bound to arise. Aurin tells us the same thing here, with the Dominion-folk. She paints them as infiltrators, savages, looking to sabotage the Kirin way of life and steal what they can from it. People are happy to believe that, and it's far easier to swallow than the idea of a counter-world, no matter what the Dominion liars might say." He tilted his head and adopted an expression to let them know he was being ironic. "I only know the truth because of Elani. I couldn't turn over a girl that young and helpless for arrest."

"I was *not* helpless!" Elani grumped, but neither of them elaborated on the situation that they were talking about.

Tochaa smiled indulgently. "Anyway, finding Elani is what set me on my . . . revolutionary kick, shall we say? We've been having the same culling of Resonants, too." He paused. "But even among those who know of both worlds, it's not common knowledge that Macaan and Aurin are related. From what I've heard, Macaan's done a good job of suppressing most of the details about himself from you in the Dominions. He and Aurin have done an even better job here."

"He would have told us," Ryushi insisted, looking to Kia for support but finding himself disappointed. "Why would he hide it?"

Elani sighed. "Cousin Ryushi, if he told us about his daughter, we'd all wonder where she *was*. And that'd lead us to Tweentime. And then we'd see what was going on here."

"What *is* going on here?" Ryushi asked the room in general, appealing to anyone for an answer.

"This place is what the Dominions will be like, a few years from now, if Macaan gets his way," Tochaa said. "Utterly subjugated under his rule."

"That's treason!" Ryushi exclaimed angrily, getting to his feet. But Tochaa sat where he was, gazing calmly up at him with his milky eyes.

"We're all traitors here," he said. "I'm sure you are less different than you imagine."

Ryushi blazed, but he remembered the creature he had killed in Elani's defense; one of the Jachyra. The King's secret police. And what about the rider he had destroyed in the sky over the mountains? He felt sick with shame and anger, but Tochaa was right. He sat down again, trembling slightly.

Tochaa tilted his head and changed the subject. "Well, you know that Kirins in general take a dim view of outlanders in their cities. You were right to come to me. If you'd have tried to get out by yourselves, the guards would have arrested you. Or worse."

"Why? What have we done?" Ryushi asked sullenly.

"Well, aside from the Princess's edict that all outlanders should be arrested on sight, Kirins don't get along with Dominion-folk, as a rule. Some fear them, some hate them, but almost all mistrust them. It works both ways, of course," he finished, with a pointed glance at Hochi, who bridled but was silent.

"Tochaa and Moracq aren't like that, though," Elani said, beaming. The old man's head raised quizzically at the mention of his name, then he went back to scribbling on his parchment.

"That's because we had to look after one of yours for so long," Tochaa said, ruffling the girl's hair.

"It doesn't make sense, though," Gerdi said, glancing from Tochaa to Hochi and sensing the tension that hovered between them. "Why should the Kirins act like that? Or the Dominion-folk?" he added.

"People fear what they don't understand," Tochaa said. "They're afraid of *difference*. It upsets them." He smiled. "Perhaps you are young enough yet to avoid falling prey to the *wisdom* of your elders." He loaded the last comment with enough sarcasm to make Hochi frown.

Too young, or too naïve, Ryushi thought bitterly, referring to himself and Kia.

"Still, you say you crossed over while still in the city?" Tochaa continued. "That's bad. The King will know, and so will the Princess, in time. We have to get you out of here fast. Leave the arrangements to me. I'll be back in a few hours." With that, he disappeared back up to the storm doors, unlocked them, and went on through, closing them behind him with a clatter.

They rested and ate while they waited for Tochaa's return. Moracq supplied them with a basket of strange fruits, a bitter-tasting and salty soup, a loaf of black bread, and a tasty and filling pie, the ingredients of which nobody dared ask in case the knowledge would spoil their enjoyment.

Ryushi, given time to himself to brood, fell into a deep depression. What was happening inside Kia's head, none but she knew, for nothing showed on her face. The tragedy of yesterday — which already seemed a hundred years ago — had left scars that were invisible to the untrained eye; and had not an observer known of her kind and vivacious spirit before the death of her father, and noticed the change that had been wrought in her, they would find it difficult to tell that anything had happened at all.

Elani shared Ryushi's fears about her adopted cousin. Kia had bottled everything up inside, where it was eating away at her, and had thrown up a glacial veneer of uncaring calmness to prevent anything else getting in. Elani herself was no stranger to death — indeed, it had dogged her almost constantly these past few years — but, even young as she was, she knew that the way Kia was going about dealing with her grief was rarely the best one. She shook her head to herself and sighed, her shoulders slumped. This was all her fault. She wouldn't blame them if they hated her.

After a time, there came a rapping on the storm doors and Moracq went to open them up. It was Tochaa.

"It's all arranged. I'll lead you to the underground weir outlet of the city, where the water we don't use flows out and is piped back to the river. I've called in some favors, and one of the workers is going to arrange to have the gates open in the tunnel to let you through. Once you're out, I'll have pakpaks waiting for you. You can ride to wherever you want to go. The pakpaks will find their own way back."

"When do we go?" Kia asked.

"Now, of course," Tochaa said.

"Shouldn't we wait till nightfall?" Ryushi asked.

Tochaa looked at him in stunned amazement, then burst out laughing. "Oh, you'll *like* Kirin Taq," he said cryptically, and then headed up the stairs and out.

2

A Pebble Dropped

Tochaa had been thoughtful enough to provide transport for them through the city. It was a covered wagon of black wood, designed to carry passengers beneath its soft blue tarp. It was pulled by a team of four of the odd, semi-upright riding beasts that Ryushi had noticed before. He assumed these must be the pakpaks that Tochaa had mentioned. They had large, muscular legs, with knees facing forward instead of backward like a wyvern's, and small, vestigial front limbs. Long, thick tails snaked out behind them for balance, and their heads were broad and flattish, with side-facing eyes and blunt muzzles. Like horses in the Dominions, they appeared to be guided by reins.

Tochaa smuggled them out of the cellar and into the

wagon. Inside, there was a thin wooden bench on either side to sit on. Hochi looked doubtfully at them, considering whether they would hold his weight, then sat on the floor before Gerdi could make a smart comment. The rest piled in around him.

"Now stay quiet," Tochaa said, his face appearing at the flap in the tarp. "There's no state of emergency, so we won't get stopped, but we can hear your clumsy outlander accents a mile off." With that, he disappeared, and a moment later they felt the wagon rock as he mounted the driver's seat and they lurched into motion.

In other circumstances, Ryushi would have been disappointed at being deprived of the chance to see the sights of this alien city he had found himself in. Only a few days ago, he had been desperate to experience the outside world for himself, to explore the many wonders, like his brother Takami. But now Takami was gone, and the world had crumbled around him, and any thirst for pleasure or experience had been swamped under a tide of misery. He gazed morosely at the black boards between his feet.

Only one thing eventually roused him to talk; a question that had burned him ever since he had arrived in this strange, twilit place.

"This isn't Tusami City, is it?" he asked quietly.

It was Elani who answered. "No," she said.

"Then where are we?"

Kia looked vaguely interested, stirring next to him. Elani glanced at her nervously; she had not forgotten how Kia had brutally demanded explanations from her a few hours ago, nor that the older girl made no disguise of the fact that she blamed Elani, at least in part, for Banto's death. Elani tried to ignore her by fixing her attention on Ryushi and answering him.

"It's called Omnicaa. It's a city in the same place, but in Tweentime."

"Two cities in the same place?" Ryushi asked. "Does that happen a lot?"

"Yeah, it does. Like I said, it's all balance. Most of the time, where a lot of people settle in the Dominions, you'll get a lot of people settling in Kirin Taq, and the other way around. You wanna know why I think it is?"

"Tell me some other time," he said. Then, seeing her face fall in disappointment, he mustered a feeble smile and said: "I'm having a hard enough time taking all this in, El. Have mercy, huh?"

Nobody else spoke for the whole journey. Nobody wanted to, even if Tochaa hadn't warned them. They all had their own thoughts to wrestle with.

Hochi, for his part, spent most of his journey trying to

make sense of the betrayal of Parakka; who could have done it and why? Eventually, after reaching innumerable dead ends, he resolved to leave it to Calica. Though she was less than half his age, she was far more suited to this kind of thing.

After some time, the wagon rattled to a halt. They heard footsteps, and then Tochaa's face appeared at the tarp flap again.

"Come on out," he said.

They clambered from the wagon, and found themselves in a small courtyard, with buildings towering above them on all sides, their ornate façades punctured by oval windows. In the center of the courtyard was an archway, standing incongruously in the midst of it all, allowing entrance to a small, sloping stone building, barely big enough to fit three people inside. A gate, of the same black wood that seemed to be the norm in Omnicaa, blocked the archway; but Tochaa had a key, and he let them inside, glancing up at the windows above them to check that they were not observed.

Inside, the air was still, cool, and moist. A steep stairway at their feet led downwards. They could see, by the torchlight at the bottom, a narrow stone path next to a swiftly flowing body of water.

"Follow the path. You'll find boats," Tochaa instructed them.

Elani smiled at him. "Thanks, Uncle Tochaa."

"Come see me again," he said. "Just not *too* soon."

With that, he retreated and closed the gate. They heard the sound of it being locked behind them, and the wagon rattling off. Silence fell. Now the only way was onward.

They descended the stairs to the path, and found themselves in a spacious tunnel of green stone, with torches burning in brackets at intervals providing enough illumination to see by, but not enough to dispel the lurking patches of shadow. Their footsteps echoed away into the darkness, and the smell of damp stone and running water was in the air.

"Tusami City has something like this," Hochi said. "An underground river runs from the mountains, through the city, and out of the other side. Parakka often thought of using it, but we had a problem with the drift-gates. They keep those shut to stop refuse floating out of the city; they salvage it and melt it down in the magma derricks for gas and steam. I suppose they have something similar in Omnicaa."

"If Tochaa's as good as his word, then they'll be open

when we get there," Gerdi said, looking around warily at the shadowy corners of the tunnel. He turned to Elani. "How do you know him, anyway?"

"He's my uncle," she beamed, swinging her hands by her sides. "Just like Hochi. He looked after me for a long time, when I hid here after they first started rounding up the Resonants."

"Don't you have any *real* family?"

"I did . . ." she said, her voice suddenly becoming small and sad.

"What happened to — *ow*! Whaddya do that for?" Gerdi rubbed the arm where Hochi had punched him. Hochi made a face at him to indicate that he should shut up. Elani had gone silent, her head hung. Gerdi glanced at her, seeing her suddenly downcast, and realized that he'd hit a painful spot. He turned to Hochi and mouthed: *How was I to know?* in the torchlight. Hochi rolled his eyes.

They found the boat a little further on. It was a wide, shallow, fragile-looking craft, with a keel of black wood and purple trim, barely big enough to seat them all. There was no sail, just a pair of oars, made of the same substance as the boat. Tethered against a small knob of iron, it swayed in the current.

Gerdi looked at it doubtfully, then at Hochi, whose arms were folded over his belly. "How about you tow us, Hoch?" he suggested innocently.

"How about we use your stupid head as a rudder?" Hochi growled.

"I think you'll find there'd be a lot less water resistance on yours," Gerdi pointed out, indicating Hochi's bald skull.

"Why don't we try it out?" Elani suggested. Everybody looked at her like she was insane. She smiled faintly. "The boat, I mean. Boats over here are a lot stronger than they look."

She was right. Even with all of them in together, and Elani sitting in Ryushi's lap, the boat barely dipped in the water. They rocked a little, to be certain that they wouldn't overturn, and found it surprisingly stable. Satisfied, Gerdi untethered the boat, and Hochi took the oars. He poled off with the end of one of them, and then they were out into the current and away.

The journey downstream was made with very little effort. The boat, once pushed out into the center of the current, stayed there. There was little need for the oars, for it showed no sign of straying towards the stone bank on either side. Surrounded by the rushing and splashing of water, echoing through the hollow tunnels, they let the stream carry them.

Kia began to drowse; the exertion of creating the golem back in Tusami City had finally caught up with her, now that the tide of cold hate had ebbed. She felt very much like the boat they rode in; set adrift, carried along by strong currents that she had no control over. She longed to get the steerage of her life back. It was the most terrifying thing, to be herded onward to places she had never been, by people she had never known, to be asked to place her trust in strangers when all she wanted to do was break down for a while. She wanted to have a choice again.

There would be time. There would be sanctuary. She just hoped that Gar Jenna was as safe as Hochi made out. If Gar Jenna had been compromised, and they had to run again . . . she didn't know if she could take it. She was putting on a show of strength, but it seemed more like an act of self-persuasion than the truth. She wasn't really this hard and cold; it was just that she felt if she allowed the smallest chink of kindness or sympathy into her armour, she would fall apart.

They scarcely noticed the drift-gates until they were almost upon them. Suddenly, the tunnel dipped, the water gathered speed, and the ceiling lowered alarmingly. But Tochaa had come through for them, and the gates were open. On either side, against the walls, they could see the enormous frameworks of metal with some kind of green netting strung in between the gaps. They sailed between them unhindered, breathing an inward sigh of relief, and then the tunnel ended and they were out into the open air again.

Ryushi looked up in awe as the fresh, cool breeze began to blow around him. He hadn't seen the Kirin Taq sky in its full glory when he had been hemmed in by the city streets. Now it spread out above him, a vast canvas of purple, mauve, and blue, studded with stars in unfamiliar constellations. Presiding over all was the black sun, a dark mass surrounded by a blazing, slowly writhing corona of fiery yellow. Thin amber clouds curled across the sky, rolling lazily along.

Ahead of them, as far as the eye could see, were rolling foothills and grassland, bathed in the velvet twilight. Clumps of strange, twisted trees, like dancers frozen in impossible positions, dotted the landscape. Growing on the riverbank were clusters of darkly beautiful flowers, with fragile crystalline petals that sparkled dimly with the reflection of the water. It was all so strange; strange and ethereal and yet curiously compelling and wondrous.

There's so much I don't know, he thought. *Father, I wish you'd taught us or shown us, I wish you'd prepared us, before it got too late.*

"Over there!" Elani said, getting up in Ryushi's lap and pointing. The boat hardly even rocked with her sudden movement.

"The pakpaks?" Hochi asked, looking over his shoulder to see.

"On the left bank," Gerdi said. He looked at his hands for a minute, making a momentary calculation, then said, "Port side, I think. Is that right?"

"Never mind, I've got it," said Hochi, applying himself to the oars. He may have been fat, but he was immensely strong and muscular with it, and under his guidance the boat segued effortlessly out of the current and over to the bank. Nearby, four pakpaks were tethered to a stake in the ground. One of them was worrying fruitlessly at its reins.

They got out, happy to be back on dry land again.

"What are we supposed to do with the boat?" Hochi said, scratching the side of his neck. "We can't leave it here."

"The river goes underground again a little way upstream," Elani said. "Shove it back out."

Hochi shrugged. Since Elani had come to Parakka, he had made several trips over to the Tweentime side; but Elani had lived here in hiding for a time, and he deferred to her greater knowledge. Using one of the oars, he pushed it back into the current again. When he was satisfied that it was firmly in the grasp of the river, he flung the oar after it.

"There, now that's done," he said, as Gerdi came over with the pakpaks' reins in his hand. They seemed quite docile, and when Gerdi halted them, they began to crop the grass uninterestedly.

"I don't get this," Ryushi said, waving a hand at the odd beasts. "Why do we need these? We're out of the city now. Why doesn't El just take us back to the Dominions?"

"We've got to put some distance between us and the city, or we'll just get captured as soon as we return," Hochi said.

"I don't know how to ride these things," Kia stated.

"It's just like a horse," Elani said.

"Since when have you ridden a horse?" Ryushi asked.

"I haven't," she beamed. "But Tochaa told me once that it was just like one."

"They don't *have* horses over here," Hochi said grouchily. "How would he know?"

33

"You're not the only person I've taken across, you know," Elani said pedantically.

"They *look* calm enough," Gerdi said, casting a critical eye over them. "But there's only four."

"Obviously," said Kia. "Elani's not going to ride on her own, is she? She's too small."

"I am *not*!" Elani protested. "I *could*, too, if I wanted. But I don't. I'll ride with Hochi."

"Uh-uh," Gerdi said. "The poor animal that carries him is gonna be bow-backed enough without you as well. You'd better ride with me; I'm the lightest." He glanced at Hochi, in case a blow was forthcoming, but Hochi wasn't trying anything.

They mounted in the saddles, cantering around for a moment to get the measure of their new steeds. The pakpaks were surprisingly obliging; and as Elani had said, they were not dissimilar to horses. Ryushi and Kia looked at each other and shrugged. They reckoned they could handle it, as long as they didn't try anything too tricky. Hochi sidled his pakpak up to Gerdi, who was arranging Elani in front of him.

"Hey, boss-man. What can I — *ow*!" he cried, as Hochi unleashed a bearlike clip around his ear. He waved his arms around frantically and then fell sideways on to the ground.

"Expect the unexpected," Hochi said smugly. "Us bald guys have long memories." With that, he spurred his pakpak onward. Gerdi, muttering oaths to himself, had to face the embarrassment of Elani's laughter as he clambered up into the saddle and followed.

It had occurred to Kia that if Gar Jenna was so secret, why was Hochi glibly leading them to it? After all, she and Ryushi weren't Parakka; and they'd made no promises of secrecy, or done anything to earn his trust. But it soon became apparent that it didn't matter. The geography of this place left her completely lost; and she suspected that it would have been the same in the Dominions. She had never had practical experience of travel, and though she knew her maps well enough, she felt it would do her precious little good at the moment.

The pakpaks covered ground at an incredible pace, their long, loping strides eating up the distances, and yet the ride was surprisingly smooth. They were going too fast for conversation, and none of them was experienced enough to ride close to one another without risking a collision, so they simply resigned themselves to the run.

Ryushi lost track of time. The black sun was no good; it never seemed to move at all. At first he thought that this was just a mistake on his part, but it soon became

35

obvious, after travelling for a good few hours, that he had been correct in his supposition. The sun didn't move; it just hung there, at permanent midafternoon, casting its feeble glow across the land, barely more powerful than the full moons of the Dominions. He began to understand Tochaa's amusement when he asked if they should wait for nightfall to escape. He'd assumed, because he'd seen the sun, that it was daytime. But now he guessed that there *was* no night and day here. Only an eternal twilight.

They rested twice on their journey, each time eating from the provisions that Tochaa had supplied in the saddlebags: sticks made of plaited twists of sweetbread; pots of an unidentifiable, creamy spread that tasted vaguely of apples but which was hot on the palate; a wheel of soft cheese; and spicy delicacies that looked like twigs, which were chewed for flavor. The food was curious, but Ryushi and Kia began to get a taste for it after a time, even through their grief-dulled senses.

Sometime after their second rest, Elani told Gerdi to stop. The others reined in their mounts nearby.

"It's quite close now," she said.

Hochi harrumphed. "We'll send the pakpaks back and walk the rest. Tochaa will have these things trained to return to the spot where we leave them, so he can follow us to Gar Jenna."

"You hardly even know him!" Elani protested.

"I know that he's a Kirin," Hochi said grimly. "And I don't trust him enough to let him know where Gar Jenna is. Okay, everyone. Dismount."

They got down, and Hochi sent his pakpak away with a slap on the thigh. The others followed silently after, loping away across the grasslands.

"Besides," Gerdi pointed out. "If Elani uses her . . . y'know, *shifts* anywhere too close to Gar Jenna, the King'll know about it and come looking."

"Tochaa mentioned that before," said Kia. "Back in the city. How is the King gonna know if we cross?"

"He just knows," Elani said, shrugging.

"Remember I said we thought he had Resonants in his employ, or under his power, if he wasn't a Resonant himself?" Hochi said. "When someone crosses over, it's like a pebble dropped in water. It makes some kind of invisible ripple, which other Resonants can sense. If they can follow the ripples to the center, then they can find where the crossing occurred." He paused. "That's what Calica told me, anyway."

"We just *know*," Elani repeated impatiently. "Anyway,

it's alright. You can't tell exactly where it happened, just roughly. I'm good at covering my tracks, too. And we're a few hours away from where we're going. By the time he gets people here," she grinned, "we'll be long gone."

She looked around at the others. "Everybody ready?" she asked. They joined hands in assent. "Back we go," she said cheerily, and then they were in the Dominions.

The change was so fast that Ryushi barely had time to notice it. He had a strange feeling of pins-and-needles all across his body, he felt suddenly light; and then, in the space of an eyeblink, they were standing at the edge of a forest, squeezed between two shoulders of land that reared up on either side. The land before them was a huge, yellow-leaved bowl within the cradle of a range of hilly crags and small mountains. The sky was the mass of red-and-golds that heralded the nearing of dusk, and the air was warm and muggy.

They allowed themselves a little while to readjust, squinting in the sudden light. Eventually, Ryushi spoke, addressing nobody in particular: "What do we do if we get to Gar Jenna, and there's nothing left but ashes? What if the betrayer was someone who knew the way?"

"A person has to attain a certain level of trust within Parakka before they're shown the location of Gar Jenna," Hochi said. "A lot more are led there blindfolded or by routes that are hard to trace back. And there aren't too many people who know their way through this forest," he added, motioning at the yellow-leaved nanka trees. "It's a chance we have to take. We'll have to hope the betrayer wasn't someone close to us."

Gerdi looked at him for a moment, his face a picture of frustration. "I'm gonna *get* whoever sold us out," he declared angrily. Then he glanced over at the others, who looked tired and weary. "Are we going, then? We're gonna have to move it if we want to get there before nightfall."

"We'll get there," Hochi replied distantly. And with that, they walked into the forest and were gone.

3

No Amount of Beauty

In the sanctum of King Macaan, all was quiet. Wide, shallow bowls full of water stood on pedestals, the rare white glowstones inside dappling the dark ceiling in a cool blue light, which rippled with the undulations of the liquid surface. Standing at one end of the room was an enormous rectangular mirror, the height of many men. It was circumscribed with an ornate gold frame, wrought with curling and writhing tongues of metal that snaked away across the wall. It reflected back the watery light that fell on to its surface, making the whole room a dance of fleeting blue glimmers.

For a time, nothing moved.

Then, slowly, a ragged brown hand emerged from the mirror, long fingers wrapped in musty cloth curling around the frame. Cautiously, a rake-thin figure pulled itself through. Every inch of its flesh was swathed in tatters; belts and buckles, straps and wooden trinkets hung from its waist, and around its shoulders and neck. Its mouth was a circular grille. One eye was a flat lens, the other a small, inch-long telescope of brass.

It paused, unsure. For long seconds, there was only the sound of its odd mechanical wheezing as it breathed. Its head turned slowly, taking in every corner of the dark room. And then it paused, its telescopic eye whirring as it focused.

+++ My King +++ it said, dropping to one knee and bowing its head.

From the blackest corner of the room, where no light reached, King Macaan stepped into view. He was an imposing man, tall and lean, wearing a cloak of dark purple and clothes of black, in contrast to his shockingly white hair that fell long and straight around a small indigo stone set into his forehead. His face was striking, his features perfectly symmetrical and flawless, possessed of a strangely androgynous beauty; and his irises were of a blue so light as to be almost invisible against the whites of his eyes.

"Tatterdemalion," he said in acknowledgement. "I see you have not lost your powers of observation. Tell

41

me, I'm interested; how did you know? I made sure to conceal myself entirely from view."

+++ You had moved one of the glowstone-bowls, my King +++ came the reply from the still-kneeling figure. **+++ Not much, but enough to darken that corner so that you might hide in it. I surmised that you would be there +++**

"Very good," Macaan replied, a smile of amusement twisting his face. "You may rise."

Tatterdemalion did so, reverting to his usual hunched crouch, perpetually alert and ready to spring.

"Report," Macaan said with a wave of his hand, and then turned away, gazing into one of the rippling blue bowls of water, the light playing across his smooth features.

+++ A few Resonants still elude us +++ the other began, his flat mechanical drone interspersed with brief buzzes, clicks, and shrill stabs of feedback. **+++ The youngest, the girl Elani, escaped the sacking of Osaka Stud with two of the traitor Banto's offspring. They were sighted again in Tusami City, with members of Parakka; but we were unable to catch them before they crossed over to the city of Omnicaa, in Kirin Taq. After that, we know only that they escaped, and have crossed back to the Dominions. The girl is unusually**

skilled at covering her traces; we were unable to fix the crossing point, and the area is too large to search. We believe they were making for Gar Jenna +++

"And we can hardly hope that they were idiotic enough to cross over anywhere near the place where they were actually *going*, can we?" the King said calmly, still staring into the shifting bowl of light. "It appears we have lost them."

There was a pause. **+++ Yes, my King. But we have dealt Parakka a crippling blow, thanks to the one who betrayed them. Before, perhaps they could have threatened your plan, but now they are forced to regroup and lick their wounds +++**

"There is that," said the King. Then, sweeping his cloak, he turned back to Tatterdemalion. "And the loss of a few Resonants is of small importance to me now. I have more than enough." He raised an eyebrow. "Though I am relying on you to be sure that they do not interfere any further. A loose Resonant, especially that little girl, could become something of a thorn in my side. Don't let them become an annoyance to me. Catch the traitor's children if you can; I'll make an example of them. Then, when all this is over, we can round up the last few at our leisure."

+++ Yes, my King +++

"And don't be so quick to count out Parakka. All we have done is destroy some of their operations in Tusami City. There have long been signs that their influence spreads much further than we thought; even into Kirin Taq. While they still have Gar Jenna, they can still be a threat to me."

+++ A pity that the informer did not know anything more of the place than its name +++ Tatterdemalion observed.

"A pity," Macaan agreed. "Still, I will reward him well. I see in him the qualities of a useful ally."

+++ Yes, my King +++ came the reply, for the third time.

"Go now," the King said. "Tell your men. Watch through the mirrors. They need only to slip up once, and you will have them."

The ragged figure bowed low and left, stepping backward into the mirror. The reflective surface swallowed him up, and he was gone.

For a long while, the King stood in front of the mirror, surrounded by the dancing ripples of blue light on the walls, his head downtilted and a finger curled across his chin. Then, suddenly, his reflection faded and was replaced by another, a reflection in an identical mirror in another world. Standing there was a young woman, dressed in a simple white cotton robe with blue trimmings, tied at the waist with a blue cord. Her hair was darkest black, like raven down, and was worn in two long, thick plaits that joined the cascade of hair at her back and were held there by a wrought-silver clip. She was startlingly beautiful, slender and willowy, but her eyes held something of an icy cruelty that no amount of beauty could entirely dispel.

"Aurin," said the King, looking up.

"You sent for me, Father?" came the reply.

"Your troops are assembled?"

"Thirty cycles, maybe more," she said matter-offactly. "A month in Dominion-time."

"We will be ready on this side soon. I expect Kirin Taq to be ready also."

"You will have your troops," she replied. There was no subservience in her tone, but the proudness of a ruler. She was, after all, the Princess of Kirin Taq.

"I will rely on it," Macaan said. He paused, and then added: "Some members of Parakka escaped my assault on their safehouses in Tusami City. It is believed they got out through Omnicaa. They went undetected. This suggests that they have contacts on your side. Perhaps they have been recruiting? It would not be . . . convenient at this time to have a branch of Parakka stirring trouble in Kirin Taq."

The other's gaze was cool. "I will look into it," she said.

"Good. Until next we speak, then."

"Until then."

The reflection wavered, the Princess's beauty becoming transparent and finally fading altogether, being replaced again by the smooth features of King Macaan, the dappled blue light flashing all around him. He looked deeply into his own eyes for a time, then turned on his heel and left the sanctum, his footsteps gradually dwindling to nothing.

Broken Sky

Act One
Part Five

Broken Sky

1

The Threads of His Life

And then one day, Ryushi woke up in the morning, and he felt alright.

He ran a hand through his spiked blond hair, blinked a few times, and slid out from under his blankets, sitting on the edge of his bed. The beds in Gar Jenna were little more than raised wooden pallets with a goose-down mattress, but they were comfortable enough. The morning sun was streaming through the window of his small, tidy room, making a blazing rectangle on the wooden floor, warming him pleasantly.

He waited for the crushing depression to hit him. As always, the first things that came to mind as soon as he awoke were thoughts of his dead family. The destruction of Osaka Stud. The execution of his father, at the hands of the spirit-masked warrior with the long black pony-tail. The loss of Ty, who had bravely sacrificed himself to allow them to escape. All these things waited to prey on him the moment that his eyes opened in the morning. They made him sluggish, they made him cry when he was alone, they made him frustrated and lost and lonely. They had done so for a long while now.

But this morning, nothing happened.

Oh, the thoughts came, as always. He pictured again the sight of his father, Banto, as they flew over him on the wyvern. He saw again the moment when his father's eyes filled with tears of pride, seeing his children's escape, and their gazes locked in the last look they would ever share. But this morning, *this* morning, they were merely pictures in his head. They had no power over him. They could not stir his grief anymore; his well had at last run dry.

He hardly dared to believe it. It had seemed to him that the agony would never end, that he had been cursed to live the rest of his life in anguish. Tentatively, as if testing this fragile new feeling too far might shatter it, he let his mind roam over the field of his memories. He recalled the homely smile of Aunt Susa, the taste of her sevenberry cakes. He remembered the chatter of the cococos in the kuja trees where he and Kia used to practice mock-combat.

He thought of his father's broad smile and hearty laugh. And though he felt sorrow at their loss, it was as if it was held at a distance. The memories could no longer sadden him, unless he let them.

He stood up and dressed slowly, then walked to the door of his room. Pushing it open, he stepped out on to the narrow wooden balcony outside that ran away to his left and right, hugging the cliff wall. Beneath him and above him, bathing in the sun, was Gar Jenna.

It was situated in a wide ravine in the forest, an enormous gash in the land between two tree-crowded hills. As a work of improvised architecture, it was a masterpiece: an entire village, built along the sides of a canyon. Balconies, walkways, and gantries were affixed to the walls or strung from support beams. Wide, semicircular platforms jutted out from the rock, which served as gathering-places for the inhabitants. Other, longer platforms were arranged in irregular rows, and small huts and other constructions were built on them, gripping the canyon sides. Rope bridges spanned the crevasse at its narrowest points. At the bottom, sparkling in the morning light, a fast-flowing river ran.

On Ryushi's own balcony were three huts, of which his was the centermost. They were single-room affairs, little more than a comfortable place to sleep with a chest to store possessions, but it felt good to have a space that he could call his own. He looked up at the sun, feeling the warmth on his face. The canyon was wider at one end, so it caught the sunshine for most of the day. When the false leaf-netting was drawn over the top by the complex system of pulleys that operated above, the canyon was invisible from the air, just another part of the massive, featureless nanka forest that was cradled between the arms of the mountains. But most of the time, when the lookouts gave the all-clear, it was like this, open to the sky.

And it felt glorious. Ryushi looked out over this place where he had been brought, and he knew he was safe. He squinted at the bright morning, and suddenly he felt irrationally happy. A smile spread across his face, and he couldn't stop it. Suddenly, it was so good just to be *alive.*

The days of mourning were over, he vowed. It was time to pick up the threads of his life, and take possession of it again.

"Hi, El. Hey, everyone," Ryushi said as he sat down at the table in the longhouse. It was the largest construction in the canyon, resting on a great wooden platform along a flat section of the rock wall. Inside, the air was filled with the clack and chime of cutlery and the babble of voices. Maybe four hundred people or so lived in Gar Jenna, and almost all of them were here now, enjoying breakfast.

Elani looked warily at Ryushi, fearing a trick. His buoyant entrance seemed incongruous with his previous black mood.

"You're looking spry today," Kia observed.

He shrugged and dug into his food: butter-fried mushrooms, eggs, and gammon. Elani and Kia exchanged glances. After a moment he looked up at them, realizing they were peering curiously at him.

"What?" he asked.

"Nothing," Kia said dismissively, returning to her own food.

Kia's reaction brought Ryushi down to earth a little. His twin had gotten better over the weeks they had been living at Gar Jenna, but she was still a long way from the sister he remembered. She had a harder edge now, a way of snapping at him sometimes that she never did before, and she still got this *look* in her eye whenever the King or his troops were mentioned. Her dogged progress at battle practice was winning her admirers among the younger members of Parakka, but she held herself aloof from everyone. She would let nobody get near enough to hurt her again. The thought of allowing another person to become close, and then for them to die too, was terrifying to her. She couldn't do it. Not after losing her parents and Ty.

Ryushi's musing was interrupted by the sight of Calica, coming away from the food queue where the cooks were ladling from great cauldrons or picking strips of meat from beds of smooth rocks that were heated to near-cracking point by fires beneath. He hailed her as she looked around for somewhere to sit; she frowned at him, puzzled for a moment, and then came over.

"You're looking spry today," she said as she sat down, repeating exactly Kia's words of a few moments ago. Elani giggled.

"Do you *have* to do that?" Ryushi grinned.

"Do what? Did I do it again?" she said, spying the dancing glimmer of amusement in Elani's eyes.

Calica, like almost every other denizen of the Dominions, had been given spirit-stones at her birth ceremony: her *pah'nu'kah*. These stones were implanted in the flesh of her back, along her spine. The color of the stones governed the power that they conveyed through the owner. Calica's were a milky white; a rare and precious variant that bestowed an unusual ability upon her. She was psychometric: that was, she could sense things that happened in the past merely by being in contact with a relevant place or an object. Often, it happened unconsciously; and she found herself repeating what others had said only a short while before.

"So what is it?" she pressed Ryushi. "What's got you so high this morning?"

"I'm not *high*," he said. "It's just that since you've known me, I've always been low. It's all relative. What's the big deal, anyway? Can't a guy be happy once in a while?"

"It's just good to see you smiling," Calica said.

Ryushi, a little embarrassed, returned his attention to his plate. He couldn't help feeling a little in awe of Calica. Barely a single winter older than him, she was already the head of the Tusami City chapter of Parakka. Hochi had told them that age meant nothing in Gar Jenna; people were judged on their actions, not their experience. Calica was proof of that. It was evident in the way the others treated her, with a friendly respect and deference that was an indication of the faith they had in her.

Ryushi meant to ask her about it sometime, how she had got to where she was, but it seemed that there was never the opportunity. They were always busy in Gar Jenna. Everyone was expected to pitch in, whether it be at wood-gathering, drawing up water from the river below, or helping to hunt the forest wildlife for food. And then there was schooling, battle-training, practice in the use of their spirit-stones; all things that Hochi had insisted they participate in, even if they decided not to stay. It would keep their mind off their troubles, he had said. And he had been right. There was no time to brood long in Gar Jenna.

As the headquarters of Parakka, the place had a con-stantly shifting workforce, different groups moving around as they were assigned to and brought back from various missions. Ryushi saw the evidence of many schemes and plans and projects — for which workers were drafted in and out as needed — but he only caught glimpses of one aspect of them and could never guess what they would be when complete. Here, poor mem-bers could be schooled and trained and fed for free. From this place, the movements of the many and far-flung chapters of Parakka were coordinated. It was all done under the guiding mind of the Council, and over-seen by Otomo, the Keeper Elect of Gar Jenna.

"So what are you guys up to today?" Calica asked, bringing Ryushi out of his thoughts.

"*I'm* gonna go out in the forest and pick berries," Elani said proudly, before anyone else could answer.

Calica smiled, her olive eyes flicking to Ryushi. "What about you?"

"If you wait till after morning practice, I'll go with you, Elani," he said.

Elani looked a little nervous at the prospect. She still wasn't sure about Ryushi's sudden change of mood, and thought it might be a trap. After all, she had been indirectly responsible for all of his miseries, and even though Ryushi had never seemed to blame her, it was a fact that she was acutely aware of.

"Ooookay," she said at length, uncertainty evident in her voice.

"I'd have thought you'd have gone out with the hunting parties," Calica teased. "Six spirit-stones would bring down anything short of a mountain; I'm sure you could handle something like, say, a couple of *boars*."

Ryushi gave her a look. Calica knew as well as everyone that last time he'd gone out with the hunting party, a pair of wild pigs had surprised him. He'd reacted by instinctively unleashing the power of his spirit-stones, and succeeded in obliterating the animals, along with a large chunk of forestland. The hunting party had politely refused to take him along again.

"How about you, Kia?" Calica continued.

"Battle practice," Kia returned shortly.

"What, all day?" Calica asked, mildly surprised.

Kia nodded, not looking up from her plate. "All day. Except when they need me to help with the building work."

Gar Jenna was constantly being expanded — new huts and platforms to be built and strengthened, shelters and fortifications to be made — and Kia's talent for manipulating the earth and rocks had quickly led to her being requested for construction duty. She was known as a strong, if quiet, worker; and though most of the men there had twice her experience, they generally had only half as many spirit-stones, and they had to respect her natural ability at creating stable and solid constructions.

Calica subsided. Kia's tone nowadays tended not to foster conversation.

His own battle practice over, Ryushi wandered into the forest with Elani. She seemed to have forgotten her misgivings of earlier, and was now perfectly happy to have him along. She usually wasn't allowed to leave Gar

Jenna without an escort, and she had decided that she preferred one of her adopted "cousins" to somebody who she didn't know. Ryushi had promised Calica that he'd keep an eye on her.

He ambled alongside Elani, feeling the sun through the leaf canopy on his face, hearing the chattering of the forest as if for the first time, watching the soft stirring of the thin yellow leaves of the nanka trees. Before, the beauty of this place had fallen on dulled senses; but now, he was content to bask in it, occasionally stooping to gather the sweet blue berries of the yuki bushes, and listening to Elani crow about how she picked ten berries for every one of his.

"Why did you want to come along with me, Cousin Ryushi?" she asked suddenly, out of nowhere.

Ryushi frowned, not breaking stride. "I just did," he said, after a while.

"Is it 'cause you've been ignoring me?" she continued, her tone not in the faintest bit accusatory. Just curious.

"I haven't been *ignoring* you," he said, surprised into laughing.

"So what do you call it when you don't speak to someone for days, then?" she asked innocently.

Ryushi ran his hand through his blond shock of quills. "Preoccupation," he said.

"Uh?" Elani said, not understanding the word. It was weird; sometimes she was so mature, far beyond her years, and then every so often she would come out with something that would remind Ryushi he was talking to a little girl half his age.

"I had other things on my mind," he said, kicking a loose stone along the ground in front of him.

"But is that why?"

"Why what?"

"Why you came *along* today?" Elani asked exasperatedly, bringing the question around full circle. Ryushi was getting confused.

"Look, I felt bad, okay?" he said. "I know you think that some of this is your fault, and that I blame you for it. I don't. What happened to Father . . . it wasn't you who did that. I don't hold you responsible."

"Kia does," Elani said, her voice small.

"I think . . ." Ryushi began, stopped, and started again. "I think Kia's having a lot of trouble getting to grips with this whole thing. She'll come around. She just took it harder than me, that's all. Not on the outside. On the inside. You get it?"

"I know," said Elani, dejectedly kicking the stone as it bounced into her path.

"Yeah, I guess you do," he said. "I think Calica's not the only one around here with *uncanny perceptions*." He said this last in an exaggeratedly spooky voice, which made Elani giggle.

"Seriously, though," he said. "What is the deal with you? Look, there's a log over here, we can rest for a bit. I know that people have been avoiding giving me details on purpose, 'cause they didn't want me worried, and I was fine with that for a while. But now I want to know."

"I don't —" she began, but Ryushi stopped and put a hand on her shoulder.

"I think you owe me that much," he said, looking into her eyes. There was a silence between them for a second. To an ordinary eight-winter child, his tone would have been perhaps a little harsh. Elani was anything but ordinary.

"Why's everyone so *mean* to me, anyway?" she huffed, kicking the stone that they had been tapping along into the undergrowth. She stomped over to where an old, fallen tree lay at the side of the path, hollowed out by bole-moles. Clambering up on to the log, she placed her basket of berries aside and sat with her arms crossed. Ryushi sat next to her. She tapped her heels irritably against the log, looking distracted for a moment; then she looked back at him.

"So what do you want to know?" she prompted grumpily.

"I dunno . . . Let's start with how you do that thing . . . you call it *shifting*?"

Elani thought for a moment, chewing a strand of her fine black hair. After a moment she said: "It just *happens*. I don't know how. I just do it. I mean, I don't have any spirit-stones like everyone else's got. I gotta do *something*."

"No spirit-stones? Why?"

"Can't put spirit-stones in a Resonant. My mother told me that. That's how they knew. Like, that I was a Resonant."

"Your mother?" Ryushi asked, knowing that he was stepping into tender territory but driven onward by his desire to know.

"She died," Elani said. It was pretty much the answer that Ryushi had expected, but the matter-of-fact tone of voice still surprised him.

"Sorry," he said. He didn't intend to press her any further, but Elani went on anyway, swinging her heels as she spoke.

"The Guardsmen came to my village looking for me. I didn't know then, about what the King was doing. Hochi says that I must have been one of the first Resonants they tried to round up, 'cause they used the Guardsmen instead of the Jachyra like they do now. They wanted to take me, but my mother said no." She paused, and took a shuddering sigh. "I got away," she said. Ryushi didn't need to be told what must have happened to the village she left behind.

"Anyway," she continued, "that was a while ago, near the start of my sixth winter. I went over to Tweentime, 'cause I thought I could hide there. But it was just as bad. The Princess had made it real hard for outlanders like me to live there, and *she* was hunting Resonants too, 'cause Kirins can be Resonants as well. Then I got found by Tochaa." She smiled at the memory. "I was sleeping in a ditch near Omnicaa. He'd never known the truth about the Dominions before he saw me, and found that I wasn't a pirate or whatever." Her face darkened a little. "The Princess keeps a tight rein there."

Then the shadow passed, and she sighed. "Anyway, it got him angry, I think, even though he's always calm and never shows it. He started trying to work out ways he could . . . I think he said 'better the situation in Kirin Taq' or something, I dunno. I stayed with him for a season, keeping out of sight mostly, and then I crossed back and moved around a bit in spring, till it got cold again, and that's all, really. Before I left, Tochaa had told me to come back and find him if I ever ran into anyone who looked like they were as unsatisfied —"

"*Dis*satisfied," Ryushi corrected automatically.

"Whatever," she continued, not missing a beat. "As dissatisfied as him. So when I met Hochi, I took him over to Tweentime and introduced him to Tochaa. I don't think Hochi liked him very much, but they were both interested in starting a branch of Parakka over there, so Hochi kinda forced himself to get on with him. Then we went back to the Dominions, and after a while, when the Jachyra came sniffing around for Resonants, he took me to your place, 'cause he said it was safer." She shrugged. "Pretty boring, really."

But Ryushi could tell that the little girl was downplaying her experiences, because she didn't want to talk about them in any more detail than she had to. There was more in what she hadn't said than in what she had. A little girl of six winters, surviving and staying hidden for two years in a world in which she was both alone and hunted . . . it was an incredible feat. The price she had paid for her survival was her childhood; she had grown up fast and hard. There must have been many more people looking after her whom she had not mentioned; after all, if Tochaa only looked after her for a season and Hochi for about the same, that accounted for only a quarter of the two years since her parents had been killed. She made no mention of why she did not stay in any one place for too long, but Ryushi could guess. She feared that what had happened to her family would happen to her protectors. Maybe it had. Maybe more than once.

Certainly, it had happened to *his* family.

He sighed, and put a brotherly arm around her shoulder. No wonder she seemed such a strange combination of naïveté and maturity. No wonder she attached herself so fast to strangers, adopting them as her "uncles" and "cousins." She had probably seen more places and more horrors in two years than the average person would in a lifetime. In that moment, he felt a strong kinship with the younger girl. Both of them had suffered similar fates; but whereas her journey into the unknown had started long ago, his was just beginnning.

"I don't want you to go, Cousin Ryushi," she said.

"What makes you think I'll go?" he said.

"You don't hate the King like we do," she said. "You don't want to join Parakka."

He inwardly flinched at her treasonous words, a lifetime of conditioning making the reaction an instinct. He looked down at the ground, stirring leaves and twigs with the toe of his boot.

"I don't know. It's too early," he said.

"Kia hates him," Elani said, as if that was a plus point.

"Kia wants to hit back," he replied.

"Don't *you*?" she asked.

"It's not . . . as *easy* as that," he said. "I can't believe . . . I mean, there could be a hundred reasons for what happened. What if it was a general, acting alone? What if it was . . . the one with the spirit mask? Nothing to do with the King at all, acting without orders? I can't just dedicate my life to serving a cause if I don't know that that cause is . . . *right*."

There was a long silence, during which they both thought over what he'd said.

"You're scared, then," Elani stated.

"Of course I'm *scared*," he snapped, then caught himself. "Don't tell anyone I said that."

"Who, like Calica?"

"What does *that* mean?"

Elani smiled impishly. "Nothing."

"What? You think I . . . what?"

"You like her, don't you?"

"Everyone likes her."

"Not like *you* do."

Ryushi was surprised into laughing. "El, if anything I'm *scared* of her. She's got such a . . . a powerful character, I guess. I don't like her like that." He caught Elani's skeptical glance. "Honest, El, I swear. I really don't."

Elani shrugged, dismissing it. "Okay," she piped.

Ryushi turned to look back over the forest. "I can't believe I'm getting drilled by a cousin who's half as old as me."

Elani blinked. "What did you call me?" she said tentatively.

"Cousin," said Ryushi, looking at her.

"Cousin?" she queried hopefully, smiling.

"Cousin."

2

The Slow Road to Awakening

Once he had begun to take an interest again in the events around him, Ryushi realized how much had been going on during the weeks he had spent submerged in gloom. Calica supplied him with most of the information he needed, glad that he was getting involved; but she warned him that she could not reveal the finer details to non-Parakka, and he was forced to be content with that.

Spies had been sent out, and networks of informants were being dredged, to try to discover exactly what had happened at Osaka Stud and Tusami City. The identity of their betrayer, or even if they had been betrayed at all, was a matter of paramount importance. Nobody knew what had become of those who were captured during the raid on Osaka Stud. It was vital to know where the supplies that had been seized from the safehouses in Tusami City had gone. If anything could be salvaged from the disaster, then they had to at least try.

That was by no means all, however. They still knew almost nothing of King Macaan's reasons for rounding up the Resonants. Calica spoke also of strange constructions that had appeared at certain places around the Dominions. They had first been reported over a winter ago, when they seemed to have risen out of the ground in the space of a mere few weeks, but since then there had been no revelation as to their purpose. It was known only that the King's men guarded them night and day, and that nothing and no one was allowed to get near. These things had to be investigated and accounted for, and contingency plans made to deal with them.

"The King is planning something," Calica said to Ryushi, her olive eyes serious in the orange-gold frame of her hair. "We believe that this is what he has been building up to, ever since he . . . *succeeded* to the throne."

The tone of her voice left Ryushi in no doubt that Calica thought Macaan had obtained his kingship by foul means, but he did not dare to compound her treason by drawing out the reasons why.

He saw Kia rarely now, and that worried him. Generally, the only contact they had was at mealtimes, and when they shared weapons training or practiced with their spirit-stones. The latter was what their Master called "Flow-time," after the power that ran along the ley lines beneath the earth. It was a glad surprise to Ryushi, then, when their Master announced after a particularly strenuous control exercise that he and Kia were to come with him on an expedition the next day, to practice their skills elsewhere. The chance to spend some time, even Flow-time, with his increasingly alienated twin was a welcome event.

So it was that they assembled at the brink of the Gar Jenna canyon early one morning, when the sun was still clambering over the ridge of mountains that surrounded the forest bowl, and they set out on foot through the trees, feeling the flora warm up and unfurl into life around them.

Their Master was Ogara-jin, an old man of many winters with long white hair and a moustache and beard that fell to his waist. The top of his head was bald from age, and he walked with the aid of a gnarled staff; but beneath the frail body and light, silken purple robes beat the heart of a true teacher, and his knowledge in the use and training of spirit-stones was unparalleled in Ryushi's limited experience. And his experience was more limited than he often liked to admit; upon hearing the name of their Master for the first time, he had remarked to Kia that it was uncannily similar to that of their childhood Master, Zu-jin. Only later did he discover that the suffix -jin was bestowed on all teachers of the Flow.

Ryushi had hoped for a private conversation with his sister during the journey, but those hopes were dashed from the start. Ogara-jin insisted they walk on either side of him and attend to his instruction.

"To master a weapon," he said, in a cracked and brittle voice like dead leaves, "you must understand every aspect of it. The most insignificant knowledge can hold an advantage that could mean victory. A swordmaster can wield his weapon with great skill; but a weaponsmith knows where the sword's weakest point is, can spot a flaw in the forging, and may break his opponent's weapon. For the spirit-stones, it is the same. Today, I teach you not how to use them but *why* they work."

He paused for a time, the only sound their footsteps on the forest earth and the noises of the awakening animals all around. They were used to his habit of long, pregnant silences. Ryushi suspected it was to curb his own tendency for impatience, for he had learned that every time he prompted the Master, the silence would double in length. Now he kept quiet.

"You see my hand?" he said eventually, and he held a thin, vein-laden hand out to show them. "It trembles, does it not?"

They looked. It did tremble slightly; the index finger especially. "Yes, Master," they said in unison.

"That rock also trembles," Ogara-jin said, shifting his hand to point at a jagged rock that had become overgrown with moss. "That tree trembles. The very earth at my feet trembles. They shiver. They dance."

"Why can't we see them tremble?" Kia asked, her thoughts more charitable than Ryushi's opinion of the old man's beleaguered mind.

"Because their tremors are too minute," he replied. "Each tiny particle of their being vibrates infinitesimally. To our eyes, they appear solid, unmoving. But the rocks, the trees, the sky . . . each vibrates at a different speed, a different frequency, faster than our minds can follow. Do you believe that?"

There was a hesitation. "If you say it is so, Master," Kia said.

"Or until you hear otherwise from one more learned than I," Ogara-jin advised. "Nevertheless, it is true."

Another long silence, while they digested what he had told them. Ryushi made an effort to see the tiny trembling, if only to prove the Master wrong when he said that it could not be observed. It made his eyes hurt.

"The Flow, as you already know, comes from the cycle of life. Birth and death; degradation and rebirth. Ah, but the *stones* . . . Have you ever considered why a certain color of spirit-stone confers the ability to affect a certain thing, and nothing else? Kia, you have the earth and the rocks at your command. Ryushi, you can make the very air strike down your enemy. Neither of you can do the other's work. But why?"

They did not answer. It was always something they had accepted, something everyone accepted. The color of the stones that children were given at their *pah'nu'kahs* determined their future abilities. It just *was*.

"I surmise by your silence that you do not know. Then let me tell you. A plucked string on a zither is not just a single note; it is made up of many different frequencies. The pitch of the note is the base frequency, the strongest one. But there are many other frequencies around it, vibrations in the air called harmonics. These are what makes a zither sound like a zither. Without harmonics, a drum and a bamboo flute would sound the same. There would be no difference in timbre. Do you understand?"

"Not really, Master," Ryushi confessed. He knew little about music, and this talk of frequencies and harmonics was confusing him.

"Attend to this, then," he said. "The spirit-stones in your back are stones that resonate at a certain frequency. You, Kia . . . you can use your stones with the earth and soil because the vibrations of your stones are in tune with that of the ground. You can make the particles shake, break them apart, *mold* them into shapes and forms. Ryushi, your stones allow you to create force, by agitating the tiny invisible particles that make up the air. But you are not 'tuned in' to the ground, just as Kia is not tuned in to the air. *That* is determined by the speed at which your stones resonate. However, both of you draw power from the Flow, which comes from the earth and the ley lines."

"But why are they different colors?" Kia asked.

"Different compounds make up each stone. Each has a unique color. Each affects the ability the stones confer."

"And what about El?" asked Ryushi impulsively. "What gives *her* her power?"

"Ah!" Ogara-jin said, raising a finger. "That is the great mystery of the Resonants. I do not know. Not even the great philosopher Muachi had a theory for that one. But I can tell you something: just as you can each affect substances by controlling the vibration of their component particles, so can she. Except *her* substance . . ." he paused for effect " . . . is *time*."

Ryushi's mind flew back to Elani's explanation of how the world of Kirin Taq existed between the seconds of their lives. He shook his head. It was all getting to be too much for him.

They walked for most of the morning, while Ogara-jin instructed them on the finer points of the lessons he had outlined to them. The heat was beginning to rise sharply, but under the thick shade of the trees they were sheltered from the worst of it. Occupied with listening to the Master, Ryushi had almost forgotten that they were supposed to be on an excursion until Ogara-jin suddenly cut short one of his questions by saying: "You have not yet asked where we are going."

Ryushi hesitated for a moment, about to reply, but Kia answered for him.

"You've often mentioned my brother's lack of patience, Master. This time, perhaps, he has surprised you?"

The old man allowed himself a wry smile, his aged face wrinkling. "A good answer. Now surprise *me*, Kia. Tell me where we are going."

"To Keiko Mine," she said, without hesitation. "Where they dig for spirit-stones."

Ogara-jin raised his eyebrows. "Very good. And how did you surmise that?"

Ryushi goggled at her, the same question on his own mind.

Kia's expression was bland, her pretty features neutral. "I've studied maps for the purpose of battle tactics. We've been heading west all day, and Keiko is the only town within a day's walk west. We set off early, so I guess you're intending for us to arrive just after noon, which would give us enough time to look around and be back before nightfall. Our lessons today have been to do with the way our spirit-stones work; it seems obvious that you should show us where they come from as well. And besides . . ." she paused. "I can feel the mines as we get closer."

"Really?" Ogara-jin asked, his autumn eyes glittering. "What do they feel like?"

"Like . . . emptiness. A blind spot, where there should be earth but isn't."

Ogara-jin switched his walking-staff to his other hand and sighed, coming to a halt. "We rest now, for a while," he said. They stopped with him. He looked at Kia, his gaze full of tired wisdom. "Kia, you are learning well and learning fast. I have heard how hard you train in the arts of war. You are learning to think like a warrior and a tactician. Logical. Deadly. You have become *aware*, and it shows in your words and in your abilities." There was a silence. Kia met his gaze evenly. He seemed about to say something else, but then checked himself. He walked over to a knoll to sit down.

"Thank you, Master," she said to his retreating back.

His reply drifted over his shoulder. "Are you so sure it was a compliment? Be careful, Kia. Even the greatest warriors are nothing if they have gained their prowess at the expense of their selves."

Keiko Village sweltered.

Situated in a wide volcanic dust-bowl, it stood on the bare plateau of a truncated mountain, lifted above the thick carpet of trees all around it. A narrow, winding trail, made treacherous by loose shingles and shale, led up the mountainside. Out of the shelter of the trees, the sun was scorchingly hot, unforgiving and merciless.

The three travellers labored up the steep trail, resting frequently, mere dots against the arid island in the sea of green and yellow leaves. By the time they reached the flat crater of the scabbed-over volcano in which the village lay, their clothes were plastered to their bodies with sweat.

The village itself was little more than a shanty-town, a muddled collection of wooden lean-tos, dirty tents, and propped-up shelters. The makeshift dwellings sprawled over the basin, crowding over one another in no fixed order, interspersed with ash-blackened firepits and piles of litter and refuse. In the midday sun, most of the villagers were resting in the shade of their improvised homes. As Ogara-jin and his students approached, wary eyes squinted at them from seamed, sun-browned faces.

The center of Keiko Village was the Mine. It was a low, squat bulge of smooth metal, humping in the center, like an enormous iron grub. The shanty-dwellings were thickest around it, with the villagers literally living on one another's doorstep. Market-stalls, the nearest thing to a permanent dwelling here, were clustered around the thicket of tents and shelters, and the cry of hawkers drifted to them through the sun-blasted and dusty air.

Though their arrival attracted the curious gazes of those they passed, no comment was made on the strangers' arrival. Most people, when caught staring, averted their eyes to the ground as if fearing they would be beaten. A thin, underfed child scampered along the path in front of them, his heel slicked with blood from a cut that he did not appear to notice.

It was a desperate town of desperate people. Weary folk, eking out their lives in toil and poverty. Ryushi and Kia sensed it the moment they arrived. It was in the eyes of the villagers, in the slump of their shoulders: defeat, despair. These were a crushed folk. And yet none of them would give up the terrible, arid wasteland of the plateau for the soft, cool forest only a quarter-hour's walk away.

"Why are you showing us this, Master?" Ryushi asked, feeling something clutch at his heart as he looked about.

"Why? Does there have to be a why?" the Master replied. "I am showing you where the stones come from, Ryushi. This is only one of many similar towns across the Dominions. They come from these people." He waved dismissively at them with one gnarled hand.

"But why do they stay?" Ryushi asked. "What keeps them here?"

"Perhaps you can tell me," said Ogara-jin, fixing him a hard gaze. "Not *you*, Kia," he said, holding up a hand as she drew breath to speak. He tapped Ryushi on the chest with his knotted staff. "You. But as for now . . ." he trailed off, looking around for a moment as if to get his bearings, and then set off through the jumble of dwellings. They followed, Ryushi frowning as his eyes ranged over the inhabitants of Keiko Village, horror at their condition mingled with a furious desire to get away from this terrible place. Suddenly, he did not want to be here a moment longer than was necessary.

After a short time, it became apparent that Ogara-jin was leading them towards a small, circular corral, surrounded by an uneven log fence. Inside, a few dozen people were gathered around a small stone pedestal, at which was standing a tall figure, his hair shaved in strips that followed the contours of his skull and his face covered below his fierce, dark eyes with a black leather mask. Even in this sweltering heat, he wore many layers of thick coats and furs, piled on top of one another in an untidy fashion, making his shoulders seem impossibly broad. A Deliverer.

Ryushi and Kia had never seen a *pah'nu'kah* before. The ceremony, whenever one of the women at the stud bore a child, was always conducted in Tusami City soon after the birth. The twins had not been allowed to go. But they had heard of the Deliverers; there were none who had not. Only Deliverers could conduct *pah'nu'kahs*. They appeared when they were needed, with uncanny timing, and disappeared just as quickly. It was said that a Deliverer sensed that a pregnant woman's time was due even before she did.

Nobody knew anything for sure; Deliverers were shrouded in mystery, surrounded by legend. Silent, stolid, their lives were dictated only by their calling. Folk feared and mistrusted them, but they could not be ignored; they were as much a part of the birth of a child as the conception or the pregnancy. A child born into the world with no stones for his back would lead a poor life indeed.

Ogara-jin led them closer, so that they could get a view of the stone pedestal at which the Deliverer stood. Through the assembled family, they could see that it was topped with a wide bowl of soft moss, in which a baby lay on its belly, its back rising and falling softly as it slept. It seemed to take no notice of the ceremony of which it was part.

"Drugged," Ogara-jin said softly. "To prevent the babe from moving."

As they arrived, the Deliverer was holding out one thickly gloved hand, turning his intense gaze on a lean-faced, grizzled man, who was probably forty winters but looked sixty. The man produced a pair of small, pale, egg-shaped stones and put them in the Deliverer's hand. For a moment, the Deliverer's eyes softened, and he nodded respectfully. Ryushi and Kia knew the incredible value of even a single spirit-stone; this man, in a village of such poverty, must have given his heart and soul to afford two for his child. Ryushi felt tears start to his eyes at the sight of such a tragic display of love.

"All spirit-stones start out colorless," Ogara-jin whispered to them. "Now watch."

The Deliverer closed his gloved hand around the stones, dwarfing them in his grip. For a moment he was still, his eyes closed. Above the hubbub of the town, they could faintly discern the soft hum of the Flow, rushing through his broad body. Then his hand opened once more, and there were the stones, the same shape as before, but now a deep black.

"Charcoal black," said the Master softly. "The stones of a smith. Beneath his hands, metal will be forged with an ease that no other can match."

"But how do the Deliverers choose the stone's color?" Ryushi asked. "What makes one a smith and one an archer?"

Ogara-jin smiled to himself. "Some say they can see into the future; others that they can see a baby's latent talent as it lies there and give it stones to bring this out. Only the Deliverers know for sure, my pupil. And they, I think, are not inclined to tell."

There seemed to be a slight translucency about the stones now, as if they were not quite there. Ryushi squinted, shading his eyes against the sun to look more closely, but the Deliverer was already plucking one out of his hand, holding it between his thumb and forefinger like a fine jewel. Slowly, he brought it towards the drugged child's naked pink back, as if to place it on the skin there. But his hand did not stop. It slid *inside* the skin, the stone and the fingers that held it disappearing into the body of the infant.

Ryushi had heard about the process of the *pah'nu'kah*, but nothing could prepare him for the shock that he experienced at that moment. The Deliverer's gloved hand passed into the baby as if the child were composed of nothing at all . . . and then withdrew a little, bringing the stone out so that one surface was visible through the flesh of the baby's back, and finally released the stone. Immediately, the odd translucency was gone. It nestled there, perfectly placed between the chubby shoulder blades, a black oval spirit-stone.

The process was repeated before the silent onlookers, the second stone placed a little further down the spine.

When it was done, the Deliverer took a step back. He looked at the man who had given him the stones and nodded. The man bowed. Then, silently, the Deliverer turned and walked away into the village, while the baby was gathered up into his mother's arms. Nobody followed.

"Only the Deliverer knows why the stones must be placed just so," Ogara-jin mused, as the family dispersed around them.

"But how do the *Deliverers* receive their stones?" Kia asked.

Ogara-jin bowed his head. "It is a process too terrible to contemplate," he said at length. "Perhaps the pain they suffer to become Deliverers accounts for their curious madness." He looked up. "But there is more to that story, which I may tell you another time."

Ryushi remembered something then, and it came out of his mouth almost as soon as it had flitted across his mind. "El said that you can't put stones in a Resonant, and that was how her parents knew what she was," he said. "Why is that, Master?"

The old man blinked owlishly. "The Deliverers know, and they will not place the stones in the child. Other ways have been tried. None have left the host alive. It is one of the many mysteries they carry with them." He trailed off for a moment, then his crinkled eyes fixed on his pupil. "Now, Ryushi, have you yet observed that which will answer your question?"

"Not yet, Master," Ryushi admitted.

"Then we shall walk the village until you do."

"Can we see the Mines?" Kia asked.

Ogara-jin paused lengthily, then shook his head. "I have shown you where the stones come from," he said wearily. "They come from these people, and people like them. The Mines are merely the place they go to get them."

They had wandered the village for perhaps a further quarter of an hour before Ryushi saw what Ogara-jin had been hinting at. They had happened upon a group of children, playing together at some game that he was unfamiliar with, involving a bundle of rags as a ball. In the burning heat, the children had stripped to the waist, displaying their spirit-stones clearly as they laughed and played. Their enjoyment seemed painfully out of place here, he thought; and that was when he spied it. A tiny stone, buried in the nape of the neck of one of the shorter-haired boys. He looked hard at one of the others, and saw that he had one, too. Flesh-colored, they were near-invisible, and many boys had grown their hair over it to cover it up. But each and every villager that Ryushi could see bore a similar stone.

He pointed it out to Ogara-jin. "About time," Kia muttered, uncomfortable in the afternoon sun.

"And this stone . . . why do you think they bear it?" Ogara-jin asked Ryushi.

"Is it . . . is this place some form of punishment?"

The old Master nodded slowly. "But these are not the criminals," he said. "The criminals suffer a worse fate, down in the Mine. These are the criminals' families. They are kept here for a number of generations, depending on the severity of the crime, to work on the surface, gathering the stones, polishing them and refining them. Their children, and their children's children, born into bondage. It is cruel labor."

Ryushi looked back at the children, feeling suddenly horrified. "And the little stones in their necks?"

"All stones are not spirit-stones, Ryushi. There are the bonding-stones that you both carry, and many other variants. *Those* stones are there to ensure the bearer does not escape. A power binds them to this place. As they get further away, they get weaker and weaker until . . ." he trailed off. "The stones are implanted when they are five. The method is not so gentle or skilful as the Deliverers'."

"But . . . who . . ." Ryushi began, dumbfounded. The plight of these despairing innocents dragged sharp claws across his heart.

"This is one of many such camps across the Dominions," the Master informed him, his eyes blinking lazily. "Before, the mining was done by miners."

"Before?" Ryushi asked. "Before what?"

"You know the answer to that, Ryushi. You need no reply from me. You would not believe it anyway. You need an answer from *yourself*. You have embarked on the slow road to awakening." He looked up at the sun, still high in the sky, then back at his pupils. "The lesson now is over," he said. "Let us return."

In silence, they began the long journey home to Gar Jenna. For Ryushi, the weight of the suffering he had witnessed made each step last an eternity.

3

The Final Strike

At night, the artificial leaf canopy was drawn over the canyon of Gar Jenna. The clank and creak of the pulleys and ropes that accomplished this gargantuan task were a familiar sound to those who lived in the huts that hugged the rock walls, as gradually the stars were blotted out overhead by the vast, woven blanket of leaves and hemp. It was done so that fires and lights could be used freely in the canyon below, without fear of being spotted from the air.

It was late now, and the light from a single window shone in the immense blackness of the sleeping hideaway, a square of orange light in the abyss.

Calica sat at the window, leaning her elbows on the wooden sill, her chin cupped in her hands. Her hair spilled over her shoulders, worn loose. She had combed it a hundred times tonight. She was looking across the lightless canyon. Waiting.

Her hut was the last one on her balcony. At the end of the balcony was a set of banistered stairs that ran upward to one of the wide communal platforms. In the darkness, she heard a stair creak.

"Hi, Ryushi," she said.

He stepped towards her, his features barely visible in the light from her window. "How did you know?"

She folded her arms across the sill, and patted it. "My stones don't just show me the past. Sometimes . . . sometimes I touch something and I can see what is about to happen." She turned her olive eyes on his shadowy face. "I touched this windowsill, and I saw myself leaning on it when you came to find me."

Ryushi was silent for a time. Then: "I wouldn't have come if I hadn't seen your light."

"My light wouldn't have been on if I hadn't been waiting for you. The future fulfils itself. Sometimes it works like that."

"Do you know what I'm here for?"

"No," she said.

"Can I come in?"

"I'm not sure," she said, a strange smile appearing on her lips.

"I just want to talk."

"I know."

A pause.

"Okay," she said. "Come in."

She withdrew from the window into the room. It was a tiny thing, much like Ryushi's, with a single bed, a small chest for possessions, and a glowstone in a bracket on the smooth wooden wall. There were no mirrors in Gar Jenna. Mirrors were windows for the Jachyra.

Ryushi let himself in. Calica was sitting cross-legged on her bed, wearing her blue silk night-robe. He sat down on the small chest, across the room from her. His agitation was apparent in the way he fidgeted and looked uncomfortable.

"Talk," she said simply.

"I just want to know something, that's all," he said. "I want to know why you joined Parakka."

A surprised laugh escaped her. "That's a pretty forward question. Don't you think it might be kind of personal?"

"I know, I'm sorry," he said. "But I have to know. I've been thinking all night, wandering around . . . I just have to know."

"Something's on your mind," she said. It was a statement, not a question. She could see that he was wrestling with something, even if she didn't know what.

"Ogara-jin took us to Keiko Mines today," he said. "I suspect El told him about our little conversation in the forest, and he was trying to sway me over to Parakka, but even so . . . I saw . . . some things there. Things that . . . ah, I don't *know*! I'm not sure what's true anymore." He paused, searching for the words but failing. "Please?" he begged, imploring her with his eyes. "Will you tell me?"

Calica studied him for a moment, the light tracing her cat-like cheekbones. "Alright," she said, but it was plain that she didn't like it. "Alright. My father was a retainer of the last ruler, King Oko. When Oko was deposed by Macaan, those who defended him were put to the sword, or sent to the Mines. My father was one of the lucky ones; he died in the fighting. My mother died soon after in the Mines at Juji. I was just a baby then. Our maid smuggled me out when the fighting began."

She looked at Ryushi then, a sullen fire in her eyes, as if to say: *Are you satisfied?* But he was implacable. He wanted more.

"She was taken when I was thirteen," she continued in the same flat, numb tones. "The Jachyra got her. I was watching as she was making up her face in the mirror; and the next moment, the arms reached through, dragged her in, and she was gone. I escaped. I found Parakka. I found your father." She glanced at him, taking

91

a small satisfaction from the pain she caused him in return by mentioning that word. "After that, my story and your sister's are not dissimilar. I was driven by revenge. I worked hard. I became a part of the organization. They gave me an identity, and a purpose."

"Do you still want revenge?" Ryushi asked.

"Not like Kia does, not anymore," she said. "Not so it clouds my purpose. But I want to see the reign of Macaan ended. He is a cruel King, and the people suffer under him. He takes for himself and his troops, at the expense of the people of the Dominions. And I believe that what we have seen so far is only the tip of the iceberg."

"Meaning what?"

Calica looked out of the window, at the endless darkness that threatened outside. "He is building up to something. Something terrible. He is arranging his pieces for the final strike. That is what Parakka have to prevent."

Ryushi was silent for a long moment, rubbing his hand through his quills, tapping his fingers on his head. "How did Macaan come to the throne?" he said.

Calica's gaze returned to him. "He appeared from nowhere, with an army that he must have been building in secret for years. It was a time of peace. The Dominions were prosperous. Nobody expected an attack from within. Nobody knew who he was, or how he had amassed such an army in the midst of our own country. That is one reason why we think he must be a Resonant, or have Resonants at his command. The army must have come from Kirin Taq. But how he managed to transport that amount of people . . . that we don't know." She looked down at the blue silk stretched across her lap. "Anyway, Macaan swept Oko aside easily, and replaced Oko's Knights with his Guardsmen. Since then, he's been steadily 'recruiting' for his cause. Any man-child with the blue stones of force must be given up to him to become a Guardsman or an Artillerist. If they are not, the family goes to the Mines. With everybody afraid of the Jachyra spying on them, not many people dare to resist the edict. You were one of the lucky ones; your parents never gave you up."

Ryushi refused to think about what might have happened if they had. Instead, he distracted himself with another question: "You think Macaan and Aurin are from Kirin Taq?"

"We don't know. From the rare reports of those who have seen him, we're told he has pale skin but very light eyes. Aurin looks pretty much Dominion-stock. Mixed-bloods can vary wildly in appearance, though; some look almost like purebreeds. We don't know where they came from first; they're so good at keeping even the tiniest bit of information suppressed. But we do think that Macaan probably subjugated Kirin Taq first, and then left it in his daughter's care while he moved in on the Dominions."

"And subjugated them, too," Ryushi finished. "Destroying the provinces and defeating the thanes."

"But what people don't know, what Parakka have to tell them, is that we're *not* subjugated," Calica said, suddenly animated. "Not like Kirin Taq is. Macaan rules by fear, by using the Jachyra to scare children and their parents, by pretending that he has eyes and ears everywhere so that nobody dares talk treason, even in private. But he's not as strong as he seems. And Parakka gets more members every day. The people here don't want to live under Macaan's regime, they're just too scared to *fight* it. They think they're alone, because they daren't speak out. *That's* how Macaan's beating us; by *isolating* us! Individually, we can't hurt him, but with Parakka . . ." She took a breath, realizing she had become flushed in her zeal. She brushed her hair back behind her ear and then finished, quietly: "With Parakka, we can. With every day that passes, we recruit more and we get stronger. We can stop him."

"Did Macaan start the practice of sending people to the Mines?" Ryushi asked.

"My mother was one of the first to be sent there," Calica said. "Before, the mining was done by miners."

Ryushi felt chilled. Calica had perfectly echoed what Ogara-jin had said. Here, surely, he had found the answer to his question. He had known it, deep down, ever since he had seen Keiko Village; but he had not allowed himself to believe until now. The tone of Calica's voice told him that her words were truth. She had first-hand experience of the cruelty of King Macaan.

As have I, he thought to himself.

And with that realization, sixteen winters of relentless indoctrination fell away from him. Sixteen winters of being told of the greatness and glory of their King, because to speak out against him — even for a child — was treason and punishable by death. And he had believed the lies, because his father had been protecting them until the time came, when they were old enough to understand, when he would introduce them to Parakka . . . like he had done with Takami.

Who did he trust more? His father, or a King who he knew only through legends and falsehoods, and who had destroyed his home? He could make no excuses for Macaan anymore. He saw the truth at last.

"My father was Parakka," he said. "Hochi said he founded the organization."

"So was your mother," said Calica. "Both of them worked tirelessly. It was your father who took me in, when I was wandering."

Ryushi was silent again, for a time. Then: "Did you know my mother?"

"A little," she replied.

"How did she die?" he asked.

Calica's eyes fell to her lap again. "She died a hero, in the cause of Parakka."

He smiled faintly. "I think I always sort of imagined it like that," he said, then looked up at her. "Kia wants to know what happened to Mother, but she won't dare ask. I think she still believes Mother might come back one day."

"She'll find out herself, when she's ready."

There was a pause, and then Calica spoke again.

"We all owe your parents a lot. Why do you think you've been afforded so much leeway? Why do you think Hochi took you, brought you into our organization, showed you secrets we would never show to strangers? They *created* Parakka. They *gave* it to us. They made us a family, molded us to a cause. He would have wanted us to make you part of it."

"My father was a good man," Ryushi said, his eyes prickling.

"For sure," Calica agreed.

Ryushi stood up, looking down at her. For a moment, he struggled for words, and when his voice came, it was choked with emotion.

"I called him a traitor, once," he said. "I have to make it up to him."

Calica did not speak.

"I want to join Parakka," he said.

"I know," Calica replied, smiling softly.

Ryushi nodded once, then turned away and left, hurrying through the door to hide the hot tears that gathered. Calica listened to his retreating footsteps along the balcony, until they had faded entirely, and she was alone.

"You never really had a choice," she said quietly, sadly.

In the darkness, the light from the single window went out.

And so it was, that seven days from the night when Calica had sat up waiting for Ryushi, the children of Banto were sworn to the cause of Parakka. The ceremony was conducted at dawn on the largest of the communal platforms, attended by every member in Gar Jenna who could be spared from their duties. The rising cadence of the morning chorus cheeped and chittered through the canyon, and the air was still cool with the

97

memory of night. The leaf canopy had been retracted, and the first rays of the sun stirred motes of light across the assembly.

Kia and Ryushi stood in the center of the gathering, with Hochi and Calica standing next to them. To become a member of Parakka, it was necessary to be seconded by one who had already proven their loyalty. Hochi seconded Kia, with only a small measure of reluctance as he remembered her cold killing of the Guardsmen in Tusami City; Calica seconded Ryushi.

The ceremony was conducted by the Keeper Elect of Gar Jenna, Otomo. Each chapter of Parakka operated under separate leadership, with decisions being made by a council of all the chapter leaders. The overseer of Gar Jenna was a man of perhaps fifty winters, with a barrel chest and thick arms that made him look like he could outwrestle someone half his age. His face was weathered and grim, and he carried a stern look.

Kia and Ryushi had been well schooled by their seconds in the correct responses to the questions that Otomo asked them. The process was remarkably short and straightforward, with no pomp or long speeches. Finally, Otomo was handed a bowl of a blue paste by an attendant, and in this he dipped his finger and drew a symbol on each of their foreheads.

"The symbol that I now draw represents the transition you have chosen to accept," he said soberly. "You must leave behind all that you know, all that the false King has commanded you be taught. You have chosen to believe the evidence of your eyes, and to turn against the one that oppresses you. This symbol means Parakka. This symbol is your sentence of death, should you ever be discovered. Only through deposing the tyrant can you be free."

He paused, then raised his hands. "You are the children of Banto, our founder. From this day, you are Parakka!"

A great cheer went up from the platform, and Otomo stepped back to allow the crowd to congratulate their new recruits. Ryushi felt a broad grin spread across his face, and looked to his sister. She looked back at him, and slowly nodded. He felt his grin fade a little. He knew why Kia had joined, why she had always wanted to join: she hated the King, and wanted him to pay for robbing her of her father. Ryushi's feelings were not so clear, but he knew one thing. In the sound of that cheer, under the pats and congratulations, he felt like he had a family again.

"Hey, Ryushi!"

Ryushi ignored the voice. He was concentrating,

concentrating, his whole attention fixed on the small rock that stood in the center of the clearing, resting on the stump of a log. *Small*, keep it small, only let the Flow trickle through . . .

Gradually, he opened up the channel, concentrating on the rock, trying to make it move, just a little, just a —

"Whoa!" he cried, as the energy surged through him, overwhelming. He snapped it off, but too late. A bolt of concussion fired from his hand, a distorted ripple in the air that hit the stone and annihilated it, smashing the log stump to splinters and blowing away a horse-sized divot of earth. He cursed and sat down sulkily.

"Remind me not to ask you to snuff out any candles for me," Gerdi said, appearing from the trees. They were in the forest, not far from the lip of the canyon. It was where Ryushi always went to practice on his own.

"What do you want, Gerdi?" he said irritably.

Gerdi beamed and hopped over, his shock of green hair shaking as he plonked himself down next to Ryushi. "Don't start getting grumpy again. I've only just got used to you being fun."

"Sorry," Ryushi said. "I just get frustrated. What good is all this power inside me if I can't let it out for fear of destroying something or draining myself?"

"Patience and perseverance should be your watchwords," said Ogara-jin, who had suddenly appeared in Gerdi's place.

"Stop that," Ryushi said. Gerdi's trick of making people see him as someone else was disconcerting at the best of times, and Ryushi wasn't in the mood for it now.

Gerdi sighed and shrugged, getting to his feet. "Anyway, I just wanted to say, Calica wants to see you. The spies are back. She says you'll want to hear what they had to tell the Council."

"They're back?" he said, scrambling to his feet. "Take me to her!"

"What am I, your slave? Find her yourself. She's in the longhouse."

Ryushi didn't stop to reply; he sprinted off into the trees, heading back towards the canyon. Gerdi watched him go, then began to dig at the earth with his toe. "Don't *thank* me or anything," he muttered sarcastically.

Ryushi was hurrying down the reinforced stairs that descended from the lip of the canyon to the upper platforms when he caught sight of Kia, practicing her battle strokes with a bo staff on a nearby platform. He detoured to bring her the news, and even though she took it with her now-customary glacial calm, he could sense that it had sparked a flame of excitement inside her. Together, they hurried to the longhouse, where Calica was waiting.

It was strangely empty and hollow when they arrived. They were used to the longhouse being full of people eating, as they had only visited it at mealtimes before. Now, there was only Calica there, sitting near the door. She stood up as they came in, and they halted breathlessly in front of her.

"What is it?" Ryushi asked.

Calica flickered a concerned look at both of them. Ryushi was again struck by how young she was, a mere winter older than him, and how well she bore her responsibility as the leader of the dispossessed Tusami City chapter of Parakka.

"There has been news," she said. "As you know, we sent spies to find out all we could about the raid on Osaka Stud. They have returned with several pieces of information, some that concern you, some that don't. It's not usual to reveal details this sensitive to new recruits, but I felt you should know, and the Council agreed."

"What happened to the workers from home? What about our cousins? And Aunt Susa?" Ryushi blurted, unable to hold himself back.

"Most of the workers were captured, questioned, and quietly released," Calica said. "Of your cousins and family, we could find no trace." She watched Ryushi's face fall, and added: "That could be good or bad. We don't know."

"What else?" Kia demanded, sensing there was more.

"A name," Calica said. "A name I've heard you mention before. He is still being held, and we have the location of —"

"What *name*?" Kia demanded.

Calica bowed her head. "Ty," she said after a moment. "He's alive, but a prisoner."

Ryushi looked at his sister in amazement. Her mouth was open, and she seemed unable to speak. A soft whimper escaped her lips, and she almost stumbled. It was the most drastic expression of emotion he had seen her display since she had walled herself off from the world.

"Ty?" she asked, her voice small.

Calica nodded gravely.

"He saved our lives," Ryushi said. "We have to help him."

Calica smiled understandingly. "Of course," she said. "The decision has already been made to extract him. He may have information that we need. What I am asking for are volunteers to break him out."

Ryushi laughed, a short, wry bark. "Do you even have to ask? Count us in!"

Kia nodded her assent wordlessly, still stunned by what she had heard. It seemed to have hit her really *hard*, Ryushi thought.

"Then it's settled," Calica said. "You two, Hochi, Gerdi, and Elani will set out tomorrow to bring your friend back. I have to stay, to oversee reorganizing the scattered parts of the Tusami City chapter. But we've sent word to Tochaa, and he's agreed to help. We —"

"Elani?" Ryushi suddenly queried. "But surely you can't put her in danger like that!"

"She has to go," Calica said. "Ty's not being held in the Dominions at all. He's in Kirin Taq; on the prison plateau of Os Dakar. Someone needs to take you over there and bring you back."

Kia didn't care about where he was being held. Os Dakar? The name meant nothing to her. A prison plateau? What was that? It didn't matter. Wherever Ty was held, she would find him. Because suddenly, hope shone out for her, illuminating a future that she had imagined as bleak and cheerless. A chance, an opportunity to win back just *one* of the people she had lost . . . It was more than she had dreamed of.

Her fist clenched unconsciously, and she swore to herself that she would return to this place with Ty, or not return at all.

"Make what preparations you need," Calica said, her voice sounding distant to Kia's ears. "You leave at dawn."

Broken Sky

Act One
Part Six

1

Enough Times

Os Dakar brooded beneath the dark sun of Kirin Taq. It stood alone in the bleak and barren plains, an irregular platform of land that rose two hundred feet from the cracked, broken soil. Atop the plateau, dark buildings and makeshift stockades hunched among the twisted forests and shattered ridges of stone, thrown up by the violence of an earthquake long past. A high, smooth wall, jagged with shivers of spikes, encircled the plateau's edge, black and forbidding. At the base of the sheer cliffs there was a single, massive gate of iron, the metal flaking with the passage of years, blank, huge, and impassable.

"What are *they*?" whispered Elani, pointing to the angular shapes, tiny at this distance, that patrolled the perimeter of Os Dakar.

"Keriags," Tochaa replied, his lilting accent mangled by the ugliness of the word. "I suggest we *don't* tangle with them."

They were crouched in the shade of a rock overhang, where the feeble twilight of the eclipsed sun was rendered an almost total black. It was a vantage point a little way up the side of one of the small mountains that studded the otherwise featureless plains. The approach to Os Dakar provided little cover, and it was not as if they could wait till nightfall. They had travelled for the span of two days and a night, but there had been no change in the dim light, and no movement from the black orb and its blazing corona. The sun never set in Kirin Taq.

Their pakpaks were tethered nearby, tired from the long ride, silently nuzzling and sniffing one another or dipping their leathery mouths into the fodder-bags that hung around their underbellies like aprons. The Parakkans had been watching the forbidding prison for hours now, trying to formulate a plan that would get them in and out unnoticed. As yet, they had come up with nothing.

"If only for a wyvern!" Hochi exclaimed, his voice thick with frustration.

"No good," said Tochaa. He handed his spyglass to

Hochi: two spheres of magnifying glass wrapped in a cone of cured and hardened leather. "See there?" he said, directing his attention to the small shapes on the high wall that ran around the tops of the cliffs.

Hochi looked. The green-armoured uniform of the Artillerists filled his sight, sitting at long, thin force-cannons mounted on steam-driven, swivelling cupolas.

"Air defense," Tochaa said. "They'd blow us out of the sky."

Hochi handed the spyglass back to the tall, hand-some Kirin with a nod of grudging agreement. Tochaa was proving to be worth his weight in gold, that much was for certain. Having a contact such as him, with all his knowledge of his homeland, made life much eas-ier; even if Hochi could not bring himself to like or trust the unflappable rebel, he was a useful ally.

"We can't get in there! It's impossible!" Elani said, stamping her feet.

"'Course it isn't!" Gerdi told her. "I've got into and out of places a lot worse than this!"

"Really?" said Hochi, raising an eyebrow and folding his massive arms across his chest. "Name one."

"Well, alright, maybe not *worse* than this, but . . . you know you put those triple locks on the larder door back at Tusami City? And you put that stable-girl on it to guard it? Because your favorite pastries kept disappearing?"

"That was *you*?" Hochi roared.

"Natch," Gerdi said, grinning cheekily. "And just to let you know, little Yuoni was glad to let me by for a share of the profits. And those locks? Forgive the expression, Hoch, but they were child's play."

"I'll make a pastry from your *head*!" Hochi cried, lunging after the Noman boy. But Gerdi, true to form, nipped away from his grasp with a laugh, and into the shadows. Elani giggled at the spectacle, but the pakpaks shifted skittishly. Ryushi and Tochaa got a hold of the big man and waited for him to ease down. Gerdi kept his distance, a mocking smile on his face.

"Come on, we don't have time for this," Tochaa said, his disconcerting cream-on-white eyes drilling into Hochi.

"Sometimes you just gotta let those pastries go," Ryushi said sagely.

Hochi subsided, with a venomous glance at Gerdi, then turned to Tochaa. "Don't tell me what to do," he said. "I won't take orders from a Kirin." He returned his gaze again to the bleak landscape before them.

Tochaa didn't respond for a moment, and then turned away with a tired sigh. Ryushi was appalled at the big man's behavior. Was this how *all* adults were? From what Tochaa had told them, the groundless prejudice worked both ways, but even so.

It was another aspect of the world outside his sheltered home that he had never encountered until recently, but it was the one that was giving him the most problems. Why were Kirins and Dominion-folk so predisposed to hate each other? It couldn't possibly be solely on the of their skin and eyes; he couldn't imagine anything more stupid. He might as well hate Kia for being female.

After a moment, he forced the thoughts down. They would do no good here. Instead, he stepped forward to stand next to Tochaa and said: "What can we expect up there?"

"The only details I have are hardly comprehensive," he said. "And probably out of date. Not many people get out of that place."

"So tell us what you *do* know," said Kia, leaning on her bo staff. Both she and her twin had been supplied with new weapons in Gar Jenna, to replace the ones they had lost during their escape from Osaka Stud.

Tochaa put his eye to the spyglass again, talking as he studied the plateau. "As I said, an aerial assault is out of the question, even if we had the resources to stage one.

Plus, it would be impossible to get in unseen. We could try and scale the cliffs, but then we have to make it over the wall at the top. That's heavily guarded; I'm not keen on our chances. The only other way is through the gate. Inside, there's a network of tunnels and corridors that lead up to the plateau. They'll be guarded. And once we're on the plateau, well . . ." he glanced at Hochi. "That's where the real trouble will start."

"Oh, good," said Kia sarcastically. "And there I was thinking how easy it was just to get *in* there."

Tochaa gave her a look, indicating that this was no laughing matter. Nobody was laughing anyway. He returned to the spyglass and went on.

"Os Dakar's rules are simple. The prisoner is put on the plateau, and after that they have to fend for themselves. There's all kinds of dangerous creatures that live up there. The prisoners band together to survive. And surviving isn't that easy." He handed the spyglass to Elani. "You can just about see some of the stockades from here."

"Why are there so many?" Elani asked, peering through the magnifying lenses. "Why not just one, for everybody?"

"That's the beauty of the place. As if the prisoners don't have enough to worry about, they're also at war with one another. It's a constant battle to control the limited food and water and resources. They don't even have time to think about escaping. It's the most impenetrable prison in *both* worlds. Aurin and Macaan send those prisoners here whom they don't want to execute for whatever reason. For some, it's because they think death is too easy on them; for others . . . well, I don't know. But it's held by both Macaan's troops — the Guardsmen — and Aurin's, which are the Keriags. A monument to tyrant cooperation," he finished bitterly.

"What I don't get," said Gerdi, "is why we didn't just walk to where Os Dakar is on the Dominions' side and use Elani to cross over inside the walls?"

"'Cause they'd *know*, dummy," said Elani.

"Macaan's men would sense it," Hochi agreed. "They'd guess what we were up to. And then we'd have the Jachyra to deal with, on top of everything else."

"Great," said Gerdi sullenly. "So what *do* we do?"

There was silence for a moment. Then Kia stirred. She had been watching the tiny figures of the Keriags, crawling tirelessly around the base of the plateau. Now she took the spyglass out of Elani's hands and raised it to her eye. The dark shape of a Keriag sentry jumped into view. It was a terrifying sight: six armoured, chitinous legs, arranged spiderlike around the central thorax that hung low between them. The head, arms, and chest were like that of a human, except covered in a night-black, thorny epidermis; they were suspended grotesquely, disembodied, between the legs. The Keriags carried in their hands long, jagged spears called *gaer bolga*, with backward-facing serrations that could be lodged in a man's body and would rip and gouge as they were pulled out. Their faces, covered by the same horn-ridged stuff as the rest of their skin, were split by unnaturally wide mouths crammed with long, narrow needle-teeth; and their eyes, hidden under the juts of their rigid brows, glistened black.

"They always come at the same time," she observed aloud. "The sentries walk at exactly the same speed."

"Nobody's sure how the Keriag mind works," Tochaa said. "But it's been said that they're all connected . . . linked, somehow, by the same guiding mind."

"Like termites?" Kia asked.

"I suppose," Tochaa said.

She put down the spyglass. "Then I think I know a way in," she said.

On the far side of the plateau, a Keriag walked, its serrated spear held low between its long, knob-kneed legs. Its hard, hooked feet trod the packed earth with a sharp *tak-tak-tak.* Although it could not see the Keriag that patrolled ahead of it or the one behind it, due to the curvature of the plateau's rocky foot, it knew exactly where they were and kept the same pace. In this way, there was never more than a few minutes when any spot on the dusty plain that surrounded Os Dakar was not visible to one of them, and it would take four times that to cross the plain, even with a pakpak. Approach was impossible.

But then it stopped, suddenly freezing perfectly still, three of its feet hovering inches above the ground. To its right, there was an almost imperceptible stirring, a shiver in the earth that made the loose specks of dirt and pebbles jitter and bounce. It lasted for a few seconds, and then subsided. All was as it had been.

The Keriag stayed still for a few moments more, and then walked cautiously over to where the disturbance had been. Its glittering black eyes scanned the ground. Individually, it had no capacity for reason; it relied on the hive-mind to supply that facility. But the hive-mind had no answers for it. It raised its head and looked around, shifting its six legs uncertainly. Nothing moved.

It was about to resume its patrol when the ground suddenly gave way beneath it, caving in under its feet. It jerked downwards, off-balance, tipping into the sinkhole that gaped to receive it; but it never got to the bottom, for out of the pit came a golem, lunging upwards and encircling it within massive, stone-veined arms. Roaring, the golem stepped out on to flat land, carrying its thrashing victim with it, and then squeezed, crushing the insectile body in a bear hug with a loud cracking.

The hive-mind felt the mental alarm of one of its contributors a moment before the life was snuffed out, fading from the collective consciousness of the Keriags. But that moment was enough. In less than a second, the other patrolling Keriags had broken their pattern, skittering to the defense of Os Dakar.

"They're going!" said Elani, watching the small black shapes head off at speed.

"Kia? Are you okay?" Ryushi asked, observing his sister's taut expression of concentration.

"Just let me get on with it. Don't distract me," she replied, her eyes closed and her hands clenched around the pommel of her saddle. They were on their pakpaks, having followed the mountains as close as they could to the plateau without revealing themselves. But Os Dakar still seemed far too distant for comfort, and the expanse of empty plain between it and them was frighteningly large.

"They're almost out of sight," Tochaa reported, his eye pressed to the spyglass. Beneath him, his pakpak fidgeted, sensing the tension.

Ryushi gathered up the reins of his sister's mount. She would be too preoccupied to concentrate on riding; he would have to lead her pakpak from the back of his own. It would slow them down, but that couldn't be helped.

"Now!" Tochaa said, and spurred his pakpak forward. The others followed suit, breaking from the cover of the mountains and racing across the plains towards the enormous platform of land that loomed before them.

The two-toed feet of the pakpaks pounded the dry, hard earth. They ran flat out, sprinting forward to cover as much ground as possible, urged on by their riders. Their approach was not taking them towards the gate, which was the most open and therefore the most visible path across the plains. Instead, they headed for the foot of the plateau from a different angle, taking the shortest possible route, where the surrounding mountains leaned nearest. On either side of their destination, the cliffs bulged out to form a ragged promontory. It would take a little longer for the Keriags to make their way around the massive, rocky projections; and until they had rounded the corner, they would be unable to see the intruders.

Now all that mattered was how long Kia could keep up the distraction.

The decoy had relied entirely on Tochaa's suggestion that Keriag thought-processes were similar to those of termites. Kia remembered a time when she and Ty had found a termitary on a sultry summer's afternoon when they were younger, and out of idle curiosity she had poked at its walls with a long branch that she had found. She had noticed then how the tiny white creatures had swarmed to attack the invading object, moving as one to defend the colony. She had hoped that the Keriags would react in a similar way.

But she had no time to think about that now. She was only vaguely conscious of the rocking motion of the pak-pak that tore at full speed across the plains, carrying her with it. For she was in the earth, inside the golem, in every inch of its skin of dirt and mud. Its arms were her arms; its legs were her legs. But its *eyes* . . . ah, that was a different matter. Something as complex as a working eye could not be fashioned from dirt, no matter how skilful the sculptor. Kia could sense the vibrations in the ground of the Keriag's scurrying feet, but the golem's eyes were merely holes in its chest above its gaping mouth. She was blind, relying only on her vibration-sense to tell her where her enemies were. When out of her sight, she could only approximate where to swing her golem's blows, and although with practice she had become remarkably good at it — as shown by her fight with Ryushi in the forest, and the battle with the Guardsmen at the mountain market in Tusami City — it meant that what had started out as a difficult fight to win had become impossible. She couldn't hope to beat the Keriags. She could only delay them for as long as she could.

Gerdi was to handle the Artillerists, high above them. He was adept at making people see different things when they looked at him; with a little extra effort, he could deflect their attention away from him, creating a blind spot in their minds that made them simply forget about him as soon as they saw him. But now he was straining his powers to their limit, for even though they were little more than specks on the landscape, he had to try and keep the attention of the sentries off *all* of them. It was only possible because they were so distant and difficult to notice anyway; and he didn't trust his abilities to work on the alien minds of the Keriags. It seemed to be successful so far, but it was hard work. Very hard work.

They rode onward, the long, bounding steps of the pakpaks hurtling them towards the plateau. The blank walls of the cliffs rose up before them, huge and sheer, seeming to tower ever higher as they approached. No cry of alarm went up, no sight of a spiderlike black figure was glimpsed; but each of them glanced at Kia every once in a while, wondering what was happening on the other side of the plateau, wondering if she could hold out long enough for them to make it to safety.

Safety. It was a relative term, in this place.

Kia could feel the plunging strike of a Keriag's serrated spear as it sawed into her leg. Though it caused her no physical pain, it made her shudder, and she lashed a huge hand out towards where she guessed the Keriag to be. She was rewarded with a sharp impact as the clublike fist of the golem sent the Keriag flying, landing in a heap of limbs some distance away. But there were too many of them, crawling over her earthen skin, swarming up her body and plunging their *gaer bolga* in and out of her. It was becoming harder and harder to hold the golem's shape, as parts were hacked off it and regrew again and again. She flailed, occasionally connecting with a Keriag, more often missing the lightning-fast creatures as they darted around her creation.

Then, a blast of white pain. Not from the golem, but from her own self. Her concentration dissolved, and on the far side of the plateau the huge golem came apart in a landslide of dirt, collapsing under the Keriags that crawled over it. For a moment, there was only disorientation and a blazing ache in her cheek and arm and thigh on one side; and then her eyes and mind fell back into synch, and she realized what had happened. She was lying on the ground. Behind her, her pakpak thrashed and groaned and whined in pain, its tail thumping the ground. Elani was crying something: "Help it, it's hurt, help it!" Ryushi was reaching down to see to her, asking if she was okay. Tochaa and Gerdi were still in their saddles, keeping a wary eye out. At the periphery of her vision, she saw Hochi, dismounted, unhook the double-handed hammer from his belt and, his face set grimly, swing it up above his head. Elani shrieked. Kia squeezed her eyes shut as the sickening thud of the falling hammer silenced the wounded pakpak.

"Uncle Hochi! You killed it!" Elani exclaimed through her tears.

"It had broken its leg. It was dead anyway. I knew we shouldn't have tried to lead it," Hochi replied.

"Sis? Are you okay?" Ryushi repeated.

"I lost the golem," she said quietly, then, possessed by a sudden surge of strength, she got to her feet. She didn't seem to have been hurt too badly in the fall; just a few knocks. There was something far more important pressing her now. "I *lost* the *golem*!" she reiterated, louder. "The Keriags are gonna be coming back!"

"Get on my pakpak —" Ryushi started, but she cut him off.

"Forget the pakpaks, they can't carry two on one saddle, unless it's a kid like Elani," she said. "Whoever's got 'em, ride! Tochaa! *Ride!*"

She slapped the leathery flanks of Tochaa's pakpak, and it jumped into life, sprinting away. Gerdi did the same, Elani in the saddle with him. That left two pakpaks for the three of them, crabbing nervously as they sensed the urgency in their riders' voices, casting flat-eyed glances at their dead pack member.

"What are you gonna —" Ryushi said, but he was cut off again as Kia turned and started to run after Tochaa and the others.

"Get on and *ride*, you idiots!" she called over her shoulder, sprinting away across the plains. The cliffs were close now, filling their vision; it would be a long run, but she could make it. She *had* to.

"Kia!" Ryushi shouted after her, glanced back at his pakpak . . . and then ran in pursuit. If the Keriags were going to catch her, she wouldn't face them alone.

"Don't be fools! You can . . . Oh, curse it all," Hochi growled, then hefted his hammer and followed, leaving the two remaining pakpaks to nuzzle at the body of their fallen companion, making plaintive lowing sounds.

Hochi glanced nervously at the promontories as they ran. Any second, the patrol guard would be around that corner . . . any second. What had he let himself in for? Beads of sweat appeared on his bald head. Of all the bad luck, for Kia's pakpak to find a gopher-hole with its foot. Ah well, he was committed now. Thinking at speed was not his strong point, and when it came to make an instant decision, he went with his instinct. These were the children of Banto. He couldn't, in good conscience, ride away and leave them behind. Little wonder that the Kirin did, though, he thought darkly; at least Gerdi had the excuse of getting Elani to safety.

Kia's feet were thudding the soil beneath her, but her eyes barely saw the plain in front, or the steadily nearing rock wall of Os Dakar that soared overhead. She was concentrating, using the soil to gauge where the Keriags were, following their footsteps as they tapped closer and closer, eager to resume their position in the patrol. The first one would be in view any . . . moment . . . *now.*

Kia spread her hands out, still running, and an oval of soil, narrow at the nearest end, suddenly collapsed by a few feet, making a shallow pit ahead of them. She threw herself into the depression, scuffing herself on the unforgiving ground. The others followed, seeing what it was that she intended to do but not quite believing it; and Kia brought a canopy of soil close over their heads. In seconds, the only indication of their hiding place was a low, wide bump, invisible on the featureless plain.

Inside the earthen cocoon, there was light for a moment; the molten red of Kia's spirit-stones, glowing through the thin material of her top. And then it faded, and all it left was darkness. Total, complete, and utter.

They were silent.

Through the soil, as though they were underwater, the sounds from above seemed strangely amplified. They heard a tapping. Slow, rhythmic but disordered in the way that only a many-legged creature can achieve. Sinister and terrible.

Tiny, tiny gaps in the soil allowed through a little air, but not enough. They were forced to keep their breathing shallow. The taps accelerated to a run, suddenly heading away from them, and they heard the screeching of the remaining pakpaks as the Keriag slaughtered them. The footsteps stopped for a moment, then resumed, suspicious now, watchful.

If those were the mounts, where were the riders?

They were right in the path of the Keriag. As they listened, its footsteps came closer, returning, rapping hollow in their fragile coffin. *Tak-tak. Tak-tak.*

Kia was faring badly, Ryushi thought, as he heard the ragged breaths she was taking. The constant need to use her power was leaving her exhausted, after trying to maintain a golem as well. She was draining herself, not only in creating the shelter, but also in holding the earth solid above them so that it did not collapse and bury them. But there was a dogged persistence there, a steely courage that would not allow her to give up. Ty meant something special to her, he realized. He represented something. He wasn't sure what, but he could tell it was important. And Kia wanted . . . *needed* that something, to salve the aching pain of their father's death.

Then all such thoughts fell quiet. For the footsteps were getting nearer. The sharp *tak* of chitin on packed earth. Closer, closer it came. Ryushi bit his lip and hoped that it would not notice the shallow bump of their hiding place.

Then . . . a pause. The rhythm of the Keriag's footsteps clattered to a halt. Something was wrong.

Tak . . . tak . . .

Cautious, suspicious now. Right on them.

Nobody dared to breathe.

Tak . . . tak . . .

It was circling their cocoon. It had seen the newly disturbed earth.

Tak . . . tak . . .

The tension was suddenly broken by something that flashed through the roof of their hiding place, jabbing downward like a lance and burying itself. Ryushi shuddered. In the darkness, Hochi was rigid. The jagged spear of the Keriag had scythed into the ground in the gap between his upper arm and his ribs, missing him by millimeters. Nobody else could see what had happened in the darkness; their hearts had frozen in their chests.

Then there was a shifting from above, and the spear withdrew. Each of them silently braced themselves for another blow; and this one must surely hit them, for they were tightly packed together under the topsoil, only Kia's power holding it up around them . . .

But the blow never came. There was an uncertain pause, and then the *tak-tak* began again, this time hurrying a little to regain its spot in the patrol round. The Keriag was apparently satisfied that the odd lump in the earth was nothing to worry about.

Ryushi's heart began to beat again.

They broke cover the moment Kia gave the all-clear. She could feel better than any of them the vibrations of the Keriag's footsteps, and she had a good idea of where they were, and when they were out of sight. The Keriags had not yet managed to regain their patrol formation, and in the few minutes' grace they had, they sprinted across the plain, their run shaking off the loose dirt that covered them. In a short while, they had made it to the foot of the sheer rocks, where the others beckoned urgently from their hiding place.

The foot of the plateau was a jumble of folded stone, and they slipped into a deep nook that hid them from the view of the patrolling Keriags. Kia stumbled into it and slumped to the floor, gasping. Ryushi knelt next to her, putting an arm around her. She didn't fight him.

"How . . . do you *do* this to yourself?" she asked her twin. Ryushi knew she was referring to his inability to control his power when unleashed, and his tendency to drain himself totally. Now she was feeling the terrible lethargy and feebleness that came from overexerting her stones.

"It'll pass, sis," he said. "Here, eat something." He handed her a stick of the plaited sweetbread that Tochaa had brought along. She accepted it, smiling at him gratefully, and took a bite. Just for a moment, she was too exhausted to maintain her shield of ice, and Ryushi felt like they were brother and sister once again instead of the strangers they had become; but then she pulled away from him, resting her back against a rock, and said: "I just need to rest. The next bit's gonna be worse on me."

"You sure you can do it?" Hochi asked, looking up from where he was attending to Gerdi, who was equally exhausted from his efforts at keeping them unseen. Nearby, the surviving pakpaks had been tethered and muzzled and were being held by Tochaa.

Kia took a heaving breath. "Yes," she said, her voice shod with determination. Even if she killed herself trying, she could do it.

They rested, and ate, and Kia and Gerdi slept. Their hiding place seemed terribly precarious, with only a rough shoulder of stone screening them from the horrors that periodically skittered by less than a hundred feet away. But Tochaa knew a little of Keriags, and he promised them that they would not deviate from their patrol route unless they heard or saw something suspicious. As long as they were quiet, and did not show themselves, they would be alright.

Hours passed in near-silence, the only conversation in whispers, the only sound the maddening passage of the Keriags nearby, and the shifting of the pakpaks. Their nerves were taut and frayed as they sat in their narrow hiding place. Only Tochaa seemed cool, his ash-gray features set in an expression of unshakable calm.

"What are we going to do about them?" Elani whispered, thumbing at their mounts.

"There's nothing we *can* do," Hochi said. "We can't set them free; they'll give us away. And we can't take them with us."

"So what, then?"

Hochi's face was stern. "I'll deal with them, before we go inside."

Elani turned her eyes from him and was silent.

Eventually, the awakening of Kia put an end to the interminable wait. She ate again, drank some of the sevenberry wine that Hochi had brought from Gar Jenna, and readied herself. The others watched expectantly.

"Your show, sis," Ryushi murmured.

"Just remember," she said. "I've been there to carry you enough times. Now it's your turn. Don't let me down."

Her words stung. Ryushi could never get used to the harshness that she lashed him with occasionally. He told himself it was only a product of her deep-buried grief, but somehow that didn't make it hurt any the less.

She turned back to the blank face of the rock. She closed her eyes, bowed her head, and leaned her palms against the wall. Breathing. Slowly, slowly. She felt the Flow beginning to seep into her, and let it come, gradually. Building it up gently, letting it warm the stones in her back, spreading a hot glow through her stomach and chest. She felt the emptiness in the stone, where tunnels and corridors had been carved into the plateau's massive body, where there was only air. She had chosen this spot because it was where a tunnel ran up close against the wall. Not far to go, not far. But far enough.

She braced herself, and sent herself into the rock. Finding the flaws, breaking the weakest particles, rearranging, restructuring, carving a path and creating the supports to keep it open. She gritted her teeth, sweat breaking on her brow and running into her red hair. She was in the stone, she *was* the stone, she could feel every tiny part of it, and she could make those parts dance and flow like water, if she could only . . . if she could only make it . . .

"Ah!" she cried involuntarily, making them all jump.

Tochaa leaped to the edge of their hiding place to see if one of the Keriags were nearby, but they were lucky. It appeared she had not been heard.

They saw the veins standing out at the base of her neck, taut with the effort. They saw her shift her hands, so that they were no longer flat against the rock but reaching *into* it, grabbing it as if she was seizing the edges of a pair of curtains, and slowly, gradually, drawing them aside . . .

The rock bent to her will. With a low groan, it came apart. She stepped inside, forging forward, pushing the rock ahead of her. It broke and flowed aside like waves from the bow of a ship. Tochaa and Hochi breathed an oath of disbelief at the same moment, seeing her disappear into the rock, leaving a fissure behind her.

And then the rock gave way at last, and she tore it apart as if she was ripping a gauzy veil, and there, on the other side, they saw another tunnel. A man-made tunnel. They were in.

Kia had time for a faint smile of triumph before she collapsed. The last thing she felt was Ryushi catching her as she fell . . .

2

In and Out of Clarity

"Whu . . . ?"

"*Sssh* . . ."

"Whas g —"

Smothering. A hand clamps ungently over her mouth.
She tries to strain, but she can't force her body to move.
She tries to open her eyes, but she can't.

". . . heard something?" This voice is unfamiliar to
her. "Cursed things outside are restless . . . didn't see
anything?"

" . . . should I have . . . my job, like you . . ." Gerdi's
voice.

Drifting in a sea of light-headedness, her attention
sharpens as she hears him, and the words begin to make

a form of temporary sense, that crystallizes for a moment in her mind and then falls away, forgotten.

"What are you doing in the stores, anyway?" The unfamiliar voice, gruff and demanding.

"The Captain," says Gerdi, "put me on patrol down here."

"In the stores?" Disbelief.

"Says it'll teach me some manners to spend a few hours with the rats."

"What'd you do?"

"Insubordination. Told him what I thought of him." Gerdi is improvising. Faintly, Kia recalls something about the owner of that voice, something . . . that makes people see him as . . . something *other* . . . It's gone.

"Is that right?" A sort of cautious respect, now. "And what was that?"

"Sorry, friend. One charge is enough for one day."

A comradely laugh. "A man who speaks his mind but knows when to keep quiet. You'll be a rare one."

"Rarer still if I don't get out of this cursed hole soon."

Another laugh. "Well, things could be worse. You could be *up top*."

"Not for my life!"

"That's exactly what it would cost! Anyway, I can't stay. I just came in 'cause I heard a noise. Give the rats my best."

"I will."

The creaking of a door. The sense that danger has passed.

Oblivion.

"Where *you* going?"

The words, harsh and shouted, drag her reluctantly out of the cotton-ball sea of unconsciousness. Her head lolls painfully back. Her eyes peel open. The dark, stone ceiling of a corridor jogs and rolls with her vision. She shuts them again, too tired. She is being carried, she realizes. One strong arm supports her shoulder blades, the other the backs of her knees. The one who carries her is familiar to her, but she can't place him. She remembers something she said, a short while ago. Something about carrying? No, it slips away from her.

"Escorting prisoners, sir," Gerdi's voice again, speaking as a Guardsman.

"Don't think me a fool. They're not even bound. Lay down your weapons, or I'll fire."

A soft voice, suddenly filled with sinister menace.

She realizes with vague surprise that it belongs to Tochaa. "You think you are quick enough, Captain?"

A short laugh. "What do *you* think? Perhaps you can draw that knife faster that I can fire? I'd like to —"

Silence. Then a heavy slump.

"Can we hide him?" The voice of the one who is carrying her. She feels a sense of sudden gratefulness that he is here.

"Mauni's Eyes, Kirin! I didn't even see you move!" A heavy bass voice. Hochi, of course.

"We'll have to leave him."

"But he'll be found!"

"I wish I knew the way out of this cursed place!"

"Calm down, boss-man, we'll find it eventually."

"Are we going to hide him or not?"

"There's nowhere *to* hide him!"

"Cousin Kia could get us out of here," says a little girl's voice. "She can tell where the tunnels go. She said."

"Cousin Kia's not in much of a state to do anything right now." The voice of the one who carried her. They were talking about *her*, weren't they?

"Someone's coming!"

"Leave him! Let's go!"

The frantic jogging begins again, and Kia lapses back into darkness.

She is jerked awake again by the loud *whoomph* of a force-bolt, and the spray of stinging stone chips that pepper her face. This time, her mind springs sharply into focus, alerted by the presence of immediate and insistent danger. Running footsteps surround her; incoherent shouts batter her ears. Her head bounces and jerks wildly, making the muscles of her neck jab sharp needles of pain at her. Her eyes fly open, unfocused. All around her is movement, hurrying figures swaying in and out of clarity.

"We'll be alright, sis, I've got —"

Ryushi (for that is who is carrying her, she realizes) is cut short by another deafening *WHOOMPH*, and he cries out as he is blasted forward off his feet. Kia sees the flare of the concussion bolt as it hits his defenses, but the bubble of energy can't deflect enough of the force. She goes tumbling with him, and they both crash to the floor. White pain blazes all around her as her head glances off stone; but she fights to stay awake, to stay conscious, and she wins this time.

Another bolt streaks towards them; she's barely aware of it until the last second, when it suddenly erupts in front of her. Her hands fly up instinctively, but nothing hits. This time, Ryushi is ready for it, encasing them both under the protective wings of his defenses.

"Get her away!" Hochi yells, and suddenly there is a great hammer in his hand, and Tochaa is with him, appearing by their side. She catches a blurred impression of the black-armoured Guardsmen, like shining clots of darkness, rushing towards them. Elani's shriek of fright comes from somewhere nearby. It all becomes too confusing, too many images coming too fast, battering her from all sides.

A pair of arms heft her up again; Ryushi's arms, bringing her back to reality. The running begins once more, carrying her away from where the noise has turned to the crashes of hand-to-hand combat. They pass Gerdi, his crossbow thrumming. Elani hovers around them like a moth, dark eyes wide with fear.

"Get her to the gate!" Gerdi says, backing away steadily.

Yes, a gate, looming up ahead; but not like any other gate she has seen. A vast contraption of iron, comprising three concentric circles that spin around one another at a frightening speed. Less a gate, more an impassable barrier. Kia's eyes focus and unfocus disconcertingly as she tries to fix her attention on the blurring image, but she is being carried too fast and she can't keep her head still. The corridor jerks and bounces nauseatingly. Nearby, she can hear the taut *thwap* of Gerdi's crossbow, and a cry from one of the Guardsmen behind.

Now she can see a pair of crumpled black forms by the gate. Fallen Guardsmen. The gate sentries, laid out by Hochi's hammer . . .

"Gerdi! The gate controls! Help me out!" Ryushi shouts, and Gerdi rushes past them, Elani tagging close. On either side of the spinning gate is a dull metal panel, comprising a large triangular hole and a fat rectangular button beneath. Gerdi runs to one of the fallen Guardsmen, turning him over and grabbing something from his belt.

"Gotta put you down, sis," Ryushi says to her, and she is too tired to protest as he gently lowers her to the hard stone floor. He tears something off the other Guardsman, and now she can see that it is some kind of key, with a thick triangular end. Gerdi is already at the panel on the left of the whirling gate, his key ready in the lock. Now Ryushi runs to the one on the right, inserts the key and looks across the gate at the green-haired Noman boy.

"Three and go. Ready? Three . . . two . . . one . . . *turn!*"

The keys twist with a heavy *chunk* of machinery. As one, Ryushi and Gerdi slam their palms on to the buttons beneath, and steam bellows out of the gate as the brakes begin to kick in with a deafening screech. Kia flinches as a loose force-bolt flies out of nowhere and smashes into the corridor floor near her head, throwing up a blast of debris. Ryushi cries out in alarm, throwing himself back over his sister, bringing his defenses to bear on her again.

The next few moments are chaos. Fragmented images assault Kia. She is scooped up again, Ryushi's surprisingly strong arms lifting her easily. Hochi's hammer swings down, crashing into the helmet of one of the Guardsmen and sending him to the floor. Tochaa's knives are flickering. The spinning gate grinds to a halt, the steam-driven brakes gradually decelerating the three thick hoops of iron. Elani is whimpering.

"Go!" someone cries, and the world dissolves into a rush, the screech of force-bolts around her, flashing visions of her friends . . . and then Ryushi is jumping through, still with her bundled in his arms, and suddenly they are sliding, sliding, down a frictionless metal chute. Kia, defenseless, tries to draw breath to scream but can't. The chute is studded with sharp flaps of metal, blunted on one side, which flex as they slide over them, then spring back into place once they are past. Kia has time for the vague realization that they are there to prevent people getting *up* the chute, but to allow people to slide down.

She doesn't have time to think anything else. The dim twilight of outside rushes up to greet them. The chute disgorges them into the air, and for a moment they are weightless. Beneath them, she catches the glimmer of a lake, the water filling her world as they plummet towards it. She hears the hum of her brother's defenses, cocooning her, but still, she finally gathers enough strength for a scream before they hit the water.

3

Who Might Hear You

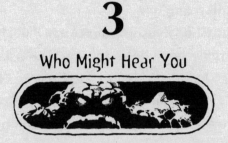

"Kia! Kia! Wake up! Hey!"

Ryushi was crouched next to his sister, patting her cheek with his palm, making her head roll over to her other shoulder. Both of them were soaking wet.

Next to him, Tochaa's eyes ranged the landscape. They were atop the plateau now, inside the massive prison walls. To their left, a thicket of stumpy, sparse trees provided a little cover. The broken arm of a small mountain lunged out of the earth ahead, and to their right there was only the cracked and lumpy fields of a rocky plain. Behind them was the lake, little more than a deep pool twenty feet below the outlet-pipe that they had fallen from. That was the only way into or out of Os

Dakar prison. It was easy to come down it, but impossible to get back up.

"We have to move. Soon," the Kirin said calmly, his pale eyes still scanning.

"I can carry her, Ryushi," said Hochi. "It'll be —"

"*I'm* carrying her," he snapped. "She asked *me*. I'm her *brother*." He turned back to Kia before Hochi could reply. "Sis? Open your eyes or something. Come on!"

A silence seemed to fall over them, as if by some unspoken mutual consent.

"Did we make it?" Kia said weakly.

A broad grin spread over Ryushi's face. "I thought we might have —"

"Did we *make* it?" she said, insistently now. She opened her eyes, fixing them on her brother, his blond quills plastered wetly to his skull.

"We've got a way to go yet, sis," he said, still grinning. "Can you walk?"

"I'll try."

He slipped his arm under hers and across her back. "Ready?"

"Something's going to see us any minute if we don't get going," Tochaa warned. "We're too exposed out here."

"Yeah, we're *coming*," Ryushi replied irritably. "Sis? You ready."

"Uh-huh."

He lifted, and she found her feet underneath him. For a moment, she wobbled and trembled like a newborn foal; but she found that she was stronger than she thought, and she soon steadied.

"That's what it's like, sis," Ryushi said. "Take it from one who knows. It's not like normal tiredness, draining your stones. You'll get your strength back soon."

"I suggest we get to somewhere less open," Tochaa said, seeing that they were ready. "We can rest there. Come on."

They deferred to him. After all, this was his world. They labored under the slowly writhing corona of his dark sun. As one, they straggled away from the lake, hurrying towards the thicket of warped trees that might screen them from view for at least a little while.

The trees folded them in their dank, cold embrace. Here, the coolness of the air turned to a chill, freezing them in their wet clothes, and droplets of water plipped incessantly from the rolled ends of the tube-shaped leaves. Elani murmured something nervously and huddled close to Tochaa's leg.

"You think they'll follow us?" Gerdi asked.

"No," Tochaa replied. "No Guardsman is suicidal enough to set foot in Os Dakar. They'll leave us. They think we can't get out."

All eyes unconsciously flickered towards Elani. On the shoulders of that small girl rested their entire hopes of ever escaping this place. She swallowed, and pretended not to notice.

"Come on," said Tochaa. "We have to get dry."

They holed up in a cave that Gerdi spotted. Its entrance was a crack beneath a huge boulder, only just wide enough for Hochi to squeeze through, but underneath that it opened out into a natural den. It was big enough to fit them all in comfortably, and once Tochaa had covered the entrance with brown moss and twigs, it was as safe a place as they could expect to find.

Hochi and Gerdi started a fire with the Kirin wood that Tochaa had brought. The strange black wood, as Ryushi had noticed before, burned with no smoke, so they had no fear of choking themselves. Working by the light of a pair of glowstones, they soon had a small blaze going, and the heat quickly began to build up in the cave until it was comfortably warm and dry. They ate, and talked, and their spirits began to return a little.

Tochaa had to urge them to stay quiet, reminding them what kind of place Os Dakar was.

"We were lucky not to have been set upon the minute we came out of the lake," he said gravely. "Something is going on, perhaps. A war between two of the settlements, or a hunt. Maybe they're distracted. But don't let it fool you. Our luck won't hold, not here. And if we're going to find Ty, we will have to go right into the heart of this place. If he's still alive at all."

There was silence at his pronouncement. Calica had made it clear before their departure that the only thing they knew of Ty was that he had been taken, alive, to Os Dakar. After that, there was nothing. They knew very little of the internal workings of the place beyond what Tochaa had already told them. He might very well be dead already.

But Kia, sitting by the fire with her arms crossed around her legs, would not believe that. And she would not allow herself to rest until she brought him back or saw his body. He was her last and only chance to salvage something from the wreck of her past. A boy who had once upon a time had a crush on her, which she had played up to mercilessly. It was a silly game, between two foolish children who had known nothing of the world, nothing of its cruelty and horror. But that silly game was the only lifeline she had to her lost happiness. What it meant to her was beyond words.

"So how do we go about finding him?" Ryushi said, after a moment.

"We start at the start, and follow where it takes us," Tochaa said. "Only in beginnings do we find the ends."

"Muachi," Hochi said, looking up. "The great philosopher. He said that."

Tochaa raised an eyebrow, his ash-grey face creasing in amusement. "You must be mistaken. Those are the words of the ancient Kirin philosopher, Baan Ju."

"Muachi was the greatest scholar of our age, Kirin," Hochi said, faintly challenging. "But he lived in the Dominions. How come you've heard his teachings in Kirin Taq?"

Tochaa laughed softly. "I tell you, those words came from Baan Ju. He was a Kirin. Perhaps it is your Muachi who learned them from *him*."

"You're *both* right," said Elani irritably, as if it were the most obvious thing in the world.

"How is that?" Hochi asked, glancing grudgingly at Tochaa.

"Muachi and Baan Ju are the same person," she said, as if she were talking to a child. "Doesn't anyone know *anything*?"

"You mean, he was a Resonant?" Tochaa asked. "But how could that be? Baan Ju was a Kirin, and Muachi was of the Dominion-folk. Which world did he come from, then? How could he change his appearance?"

"Nooo," Elani said, then tutted loudly. "He wasn't a Resonant. They were just Splitlings."

"Ah," said Tochaa, enlightenment arriving on his face. "Of course."

Ryushi glanced at the faces around the fire, and saw that nobody else wanted to expose their ignorance, so he took the plunge and did the obvious. "Splitlings?"

Elani had been waiting for that. At the prospect of displaying her knowledge, she took on an imperious and self-important tone. "Remember what I told you, that everything is balanced? Between Tweentime and the Dominions? Well, *people* are balanced, too. For every person in the Dominions, there's a person who lives in Tweentime. And the two are connected, right? Like there's an invisible string between 'em. But you never know who your Splitling is. It's just like . . . there's this bond you have with this other person. And even though you might have grown up differently, and be completely unlike each other, Splitlings start off basically the same. Kinda like soul-twins." She paused, her theory running ahead of her brain for a moment, then

149

caught herself up. "So what I reckon is, Muachi and Baan Ju were probably Splitlings. They thought alike, and they both became famous because of it. The only thing that separated 'em was time." She beamed. "Tweentime."

"So what about Resonants?" Ryushi asked.

"Oh, we don't have Splitlings," she replied blithely; then her face paused in a picture of consideration. "Maybe that's why we can flip between." She shrugged. "I dunno." There was a pause, then she added: "Anyway, it's the same with cities and so on. I said to Ryushi before, where you get one city in one world, you tend to find one in exactly the same place on the other. Like Tusami City and Omnicaa. I reckon the reason is, 'cause everything's balanced and linked, where a lot of people settle in one world, people on the other side are unconsciously drawn to it. Or something." She blinked, as if stumbling upon a sudden revelation. "Maybe it's their Splitlings?" she suggested.

"So what about Os Dakar?" asked Gerdi. "The only way out of here is to cross over, right? Won't we just pop up inside a prison place like this, except in the Dominions? I mean, we still won't be able to get out."

"Don't you think I'd have checked that?" Elani asked, exasperated. "It's all clear on the other side. See, it only happens with really *big* groups of people. And it's all to do with the geography and stuff. Omnicaa and Tusami City are both on rivers, which is good for trade, but nobody wants to live near Os Dakar; on the Dominions side, it's just plains. That's why we don't get a Gar Jenna on this side either. Not enough people, too hard to get to."

"Anyway, the point is that it won't cause us a problem getting out," Hochi said, interrupting her tirade. "We just have to keep little Elani safe."

Their very lives were in the hands of an eight-winter child, Ryushi thought. Who would have thought that the world would be like this?

Oh, Father, you were right not to tell us . . . if we'd have known all the craziness we'd meet, we never would have wanted to set foot outside Osaka Stud.

They were reluctant to forsake the sanctuary of their den, but it was something that had to be done. Tochaa advised that they keep track of the route back, in case they needed it again. Gerdi said that he would remember it. Tochaa accepted his word. It was a strange contrast, that the Kirin was perfectly willing to trust a near-stranger with his safety while Hochi could barely bring himself to turn his back on Tochaa in case he found a dagger in it.

They headed onward, following no particular direction, but always travelling the same way. The unmoving sun, hanging at exactly north-east, made it simple to navigate, and they did not fear getting lost. In fact, during the first hour or so of travel, they saw very little evidence of anything to fear at all.

"It's a lull," said Tochaa, when Ryushi mentioned this to him. "Don't be fooled. Something is amiss."

The thicket of dank trees did not cover them for long, and they found themselves scuffing along cold, sandy stone plains, hemmed in by frowning rises of land. There was no question of cover; everywhere in this place was a prime spot for an ambush. But after another hour of jumping at shadows, they began to relax a little, and to think that perhaps Tochaa's information about this place was not so reliable after all.

That was when they came across the stockade.

It reared up suddenly, encircling the waist of a low and barren hill that appeared in the gap between two granite ridges. It was surrounded by an exterior wall of beaten metal, with jagged, rusty spikes and blades bristling outwards in a formidable show of defense. The wall was high, so high that they could not see over it to what was beyond.

"Mauni's Eyes," Hochi cursed. "Look!"

They looked. And there, at one end was a terrible

rent where the huge wall had been torn aside. The metal bowed inward. Spikes were shattered and twisted, lying about like pine-needles.

All was silent. Not even a bird cried. Only the faint wind stirred.

"What could have done that?" he asked in amazement.

"Let's get closer," Gerdi suggested impetuously. When nobody checked him, he looked around in surprise. "What, nobody's gonna tell me I should be more cautious?"

"Draw your weapons," said Tochaa, setting off towards the wall.

"Alright! Score one for the kids!" Gerdi said, then ducked a swipe that Hochi casually sent his way as he passed. Those who had weapons made them ready.

The nearer they got to the imposing wall, the more obvious it became that there had been a battle here. Men and women, Kirin and Dominion-folk alike, lay dead on the rocky ground, or hung impaled on the evil spikes of the wall. Ryushi put his free hand over Elani's eyes. She pulled it away.

"Cousin Ryushi," she said, her voice somber. "I've seen worse that this before. You should put your hand over your *own* eyes."

Ryushi wished he could.

Cautiously, they went on, picking their way through the savage and casual gore of the battlefield. Judging by their appearance, most of the corpses out here seemed to belong to the same tribe, which Ryushi presumed were the attackers. Their bodies were strangely painted, with the left half of their skin dyed blue and the other red. They wore furs and belts and rags, and their heads were hairless. But among them were bodies of men and women in uniforms of some kind of smooth animal-skin, with their hair arranged in three plaited scalp-locks. The defenders, he assumed. And judging by the gaping hole in their wall, the ones who had lost.

Her bo staff at the ready, Kia was first to reach the twisted tear in the barricade. It looked like something had simply steamrollered through it, destroying the wall as if it were paper. She peered inside, saw no signs of life, and beckoned the others on.

It was only then that the full extent of the battle became clear. Buildings, once motley constructions of brick, timber, and iron, were smashed and shattered. Debris mingled with the bodies of the dead. Lifeless eyes stared at them from everywhere. This place had once been a community, an ordered and organized unit of people. Now there was nothing but the broken shells of buildings, half-standing walls that poked uselessly from the bloodied ground, and the remnants of watchtowers and balconies pitched to the stony floor.

"This place is a graveyard," Kia commented to nobody.

"What could have *done* this?" Hochi asked again.

"Something big, boss-man," said Gerdi, crouching down by the tear in the wall. "Signs are plain enough for anyone, even in light this bad. A machine, I'd guess. Tracks or wheels or something. Smashed in here, and these red-and-blue guys poured in after."

"There are hardly any of the red-and-blues inside the wall," Tochaa observed, scanning the ground. "I'd say Gerdi was right. Some of them got killed attacking the walls, but once the machine got here, it was all over. They came in and slaughtered the defenders."

Ryushi felt sickened. He had wandered away from the others, walking in an almost dreamlike daze. All this killing . . . men and women slaughtered like animals. It was horrific. His eyes took in the signs of the battle with numb acceptance. Here, a scorched spot where a firebolt had gone astray; there, the signs of an earth-mover like Kia, who had managed to form half a small golem before being cut down, the golem's upper body frozen in the earth next to his fallen corpse, a statue in the twilight of the dark sun overhead. Spirit-stones and weapons, used in equal measure; it must have been a terrible battle. Such a loss.

It was then that he became aware of a sound, just audible over the blowing of the wind. A soft, wet, smacking noise. He narrowed his eyes, concentrating on where it was coming from, but the wind foiled him. Looking around, he realized he had strayed some distance away from his companions, who were still near the hole in the barricade, looking for more clues as to what happened here. Silhouettes against the lighter darkness.

Could it be survivors? he thought urgently, sympathy overriding his desire to retreat from the sights and smells that surrounded him. *Maybe they need help.*

He went a little further up the rocky slope, treading cautiously between the bodies of the fallen. It soon became apparent that the noise he had heard was coming from a gentle dip in the land, a kink in the smooth rise of the hill; but the smashed remains of a watchtower formed a dark and jumbled barrier, obscuring his view. Now the smacking noises were louder, and there was definitely something moving on the other side.

Careful, careful, he told himself. *It might not be what you think.*

Softly, he placed one hand on the splintered wood of the fallen watchtower and began to climb the barrier. When he got to the top, he hauled himself up and looked over, and his elfin face froze in a picture of horror.

Just beneath him, piled together, were the corpses of several of the battle-dead. Crouching around them were five yellowed, spindly creatures, with long, bony limbs and ridged backs and tails. Their eyes were milky-white in the dimness and their faces were curiously beaklike, with two protruding ridges on either side of their lower jaw, and a sharp upper lip that curled over their chins. Their muzzles were stained with dark blood, and as Ryushi watched, one of them bent its head down to bite into the hand of one of the corpses.

Ryushi took in an involuntary gasp of repulsion. It was barely loud enough for him to hear, but the effect on those below was immediate. As one, their heads snapped up and they fixed him with their blank gaze. He felt ice seep into his veins. For a long moment, they were frozen like that.

Then Ryushi scrambled off the barrier and ran, and the creatures gave chase.

He was running as soon as his feet had hit the floor, hollering at the top of his voice for the others. The creatures were a heartbeat behind, springing on to and over

the barrier with powerful leaps, outpacing him easily.
He yelled again, throwing himself into a forward roll as
one of the things pounced past him, a clawed hand
swiping through the space where his head had been a
split-second ago. Springing back to his feet, he twisted
and slashed with his sword, carving a bright arc in the
twilight; but his attacker writhed away, retreating to safe
distance.

A blur of movement from behind him made him
swivel again, his sword raised in an instinctive parry.
The claw that was to have dug into the back of his head
met the edge of his blade instead with a wet *thwack*, flying off at the wrist, spraying a rill of blood across
Ryushi's face. He ducked by, ignoring the pained howl
of his attacker, desperate to reach the safety of his companions, because these creatures were too quick, he
couldn't hold out against them alone, he couldn't —

Too quick. His eyes didn't even register the third
creature in the semi-light until it was on top of him,
pouncing on him from behind a low, ragged wall, bear-
ing him to the ground. Though spindly, they were surprisingly heavy and strong. Ryushi felt the wind
knocked out of his lungs as he was slammed to the hard
earth. His eyes cleared to see the creature atop him, sil-

houetted against the dark sun, one claw raised for the kill . . .

"Get *off* him!" Kia cried, leaping over his head, her bo staff flashing down in a cruel jab that smashed into the creature's jaw and sent it scrabbling away. And suddenly the others were there with her, ploughing into the fray, holding back the creatures until Kia could help Ryushi to his feet.

"Thanks, sis," he said, shaking his head and picking up his sword. "Owe ya."

"Elani told me how you carried me through the tunnels," she said. "How you wouldn't let anyone else do it." She glanced at him and gave him a small smile. "Twins shouldn't hold each other to debts."

And just for a moment, it felt then like it had before, like things were just as they had been, that they were brother and sister once again.

"*Yeah,*" he murmured, and they threw themselves into the fray, side-by-side.

The battle was frantic. The creatures were terrifically fast, and the Parakkans found themselves desperately parrying the snapping jaws and whip-fast talons of their enemies. Hochi's hammer took one of them on the side of the head, smashing it aside; but one of its companions, the one that had lost a hand, leaped inside the arc of his swing and slashed at his broad chest. Hochi fell back, crying out as the talons missed him by a hair's breadth . . . and then Ryushi was there, to fight off the creatures before they could capitalize on the advantage. Next to him, Kia's staff lashed the air, intercepting one of them in mid-leap and sending it sprawling heavily to the ground. Behind them, Gerdi — who had stayed back to guard Elani — loosed his crossbow at one of the creatures, missing it narrowly. Tochaa's knives flashed between them, guarding and blocking, swiping and stabbing, his eyes narrow in his ashen-skinned face.

Back to back they fought, surrounding Hochi while he got back to his feet, still fending off blows with his hammer; but the remaining creatures kept coming at them with suicidal fury, screeching and slashing. Sweat ran from Kia's brow as she batted away their attacks with her bo staff. The creatures were tireless, and the defenders were not. Something was going to give . . .

And then, suddenly, a guttural snarl tore the air, and a blur of movement leaped across her field of vision, crashing into one of the creatures and taking it down. At the same moment, a flash of metal in the dim light shot towards them — a bright disc, spinning madly — and buried itself with a wet *thud* into the back of another, sending it toppling. Perceiving that they were under attack, the two remaining creatures hesitated. It was a mistake. Kia and Ryushi moved together on the same one, her staff taking its legs away, his sword meeting its neck as it fell and beheading it. The last of them, the creature with only one claw, turned and fled, leaping away from Hochi's hammer-blow and losing itself in the wrecked camp before they could stop it.

It had all been over in less than a second.

Running his hand through blood-wet hair, staining his blond quills red, Ryushi tried to take stock of what had happened. Before them, with the corpse of one of their attackers under its paws, was an enormous grey dog, fully waist-high on Tochaa. Whoever had thrown the sharp metal disc that was now embedded in the back of another corpse was nowhere to be seen. Keeping a wary eye on the dog — which was, in turn, keeping a wary eye on *them* — he scanned the close horizon of debris and ruined buildings. There were a hundred places to hide amid the ruins of the settlement, and until they were sure of their mysterious savior's intentions, they could not relax their guard.

"Who's out there?" Ryushi cried.

"I wouldn't shout that loud in Os Dakar," came a voice, and they turned to find the owner squatting on a high, half-standing wall where Ryushi could have sworn he hadn't been before. "You never know who might hear you and come looking."

About the Author

Chris Wooding was born in Leicester, England, in 1977. Besides *Broken Sky,* he is the author of *Kerosene, Crashing,* and *Endgame,* among others. He is a devout believer in bad horror movies, Anime videos, and the power of coffee. Currently he plays guitar in a band called Otherwise.

**Who is the stranger and what does
he want? There's only one way
to find out . . .**

Broken Sky

(#3)

Coming Soon

Kia sat with her back against the hard rock, her head resting on her knees, hugging herself. She was in a tiny alcove, barely big enough to stand up in, hemmed in by rough, worn stone. In front of her, a foot or so beyond her toes, a heavy iron grille cast squares of bluish light across her huddled silhouette.

Outside, the mob of tribesmen were chanting, working themselves up into a frenzy of anticipation.

The Snapper Run was at hand.

Kia felt sick. All along, when Tochaa had repeatedly warned them what a dangerous place Os Dakar was, she had paid him scant attention.

She'd been naïve. Naïve and stupid. Kia hadn't been

able to bring her stones into action fast enough to prevent her throat being cut, so she'd had little option. She'd decided to bide her time, waiting until she would have an opportunity to use her stones to escape or attack. They couldn't keep her imprisoned, not with the power she wielded.

That was when she discovered another previously unknown aspect of the real world. Damper Collars. Thin bands of strong metal, affixed around the neck, with a single ice-white stone at the throat. How they worked, she didn't know. All she knew was, that once that collar was put around her, her stones were useless. No matter how hard she tried, she could not summon a reaction from them. No Flow. Nothing.

And now she was here, in what the tribesmen called the Snapper Run. Gerdi was in a similar tiny cell, close by. She wondered what had happened to the others.

She raised her head from her knees and looked out through the bars of the grille. Out there was the arena. A vast, sheer-sided pit, pocked with small, barred alcoves similar to the one she was held in. Ledges, walkways, platforms, and pillars criss-crossed the pit from the bottom to near the top, all fashioned from stone, a multi-level maze of paths. The central point was a tall, hollow pillar, studded with fist-sized holes at even intervals up its length. At the top of this, hanging in a stone cradle, was a huge wooden vat, sloshing with gallons of foul, brackish water, in which were floating many wooden balls, each about the size of a kuja fruit. It was attached by a rope to an iron crank, out of reach on the lip of the pit.

Ringing the top of the pit were the spectators, cheering and jeering impatiently for the game to begin. Kia's gate was high up, near the top of the arena. She had not been told the rules, so she assumed that there were none. She had no idea how the game was played, or what was going to happen. She knew only that they had left her and Gerdi's weapons in the middle of the arena floor, a fair way below them, and that she was heading for them the minute her gate opened.

She flexed her shoulders. The tension in the air was mounting. Somehow, she knew: the Snapper Run was about to begin.